W9-BJL-878

EXTRA INNINGS

**Other Tiki Barber and Ronde Barber
Game Time Books**

Barber Game Time Books

EXTRA INNINGS

Tiki Barber and Ronde Barber
with Paul Mantell

A Paula Wiseman Book
Simon & Schuster Books for Young Readers
New York London Toronto Sydney New Delhi

For AJ, Chason, Riley, and Ella
—T. B.
For my three roses
—R. B.

SIMON & SCHUSTER BOOKS FOR YOUNG READERS
An imprint of Simon & Schuster Children's Publishing Division
1230 Avenue of the Americas, New York, New York 10020
This book is a work of fiction. Any references to historical events,
real people, or real places are used fictitiously. Other names, characters,
places, and events are products of the authors' imagination,
and any resemblance to actual events or places or persons,
living or dead, is entirely coincidental.
Copyright © 2014 by Tiki Barber and Ronde Barber
Jacket illustration copyright © 2014 by James W. Bennett
All rights reserved, including the right of reproduction
in whole or in part in any form.
SIMON & SCHUSTER BOOKS FOR YOUNG READERS is a trademark of
Simon & Schuster, Inc.
For information about special discounts for bulk purchases,
please contact Simon & Schuster Special Sales at 1-866-506-1949 or
business@simonandschuster.com.
The Simon & Schuster Speakers Bureau can bring authors
to your live event. For more information or to book an event,
contact the Simon & Schuster Speakers Bureau at 1-866-248-3049 or
visit our website at www.simonspeakers.com.
Book design by Hilary Zarycky
The text for this book is set in Melior.
Manufactured in the United States of America • 0114 FFG
2 4 6 8 10 9 7 5 3 1
CIP data for this book is available from the Library of Congress.
ISBN 978-1-4424-5726-3
ISBN 978-1-4424-5728-7 (eBook)

ACKNOWLEDGMENTS

The authors and publisher gratefully
thank Mark Lepselter for his help in making this book.

1

A NEW TEAM

"**. . . Kirby Puckett at the plate. . . . The pitch is** on its way . . . and he hits it high and deep! That ball is going . . . going . . ."

Tiki Barber followed the flight of the ball he'd hit as it arced its way high over Amherst Street. His identical twin, Ronde, who had been backpedaling, turned around and broke into a run, trying to catch up to the long fly.

"And that ball is . . . Aw, man, come on!"

Tiki winced and shook his head as Ronde somehow came down with the ball, did a smooth somersault, and came up flashing it in his mitt.

"Rickey Henderson's got your ball right here!" Ronde shouted. "Take that, Kirby Puckett!"

The twins were out early this morning. The school bus wasn't due for another ten minutes, it was mid-April, and the sun shone down on the streets of

Roanoke, Virginia, making it seem warmer than it really was.

Baseball season had started the week before, and the twins were already getting into following their favorite team. True, that team played in Minnesota, nowhere near Roanoke, Virginia, but Tiki and Ronde couldn't resist a team called the Twins!

Ronde lobbed the ball back in. "Hit me another one, 'Kirby', my man," he said. "And this time put a little muscle into it!"

Tiki laughed, knowing Ronde was just sweating him. "You asked for it. See if you can run this one down, 'Rickey'!"

Ronde was still getting back to his spot near the manhole cover. "Hey! Wait till I'm ready, yo!"

Tiki would have gone ahead and hit one anyway, but a car came down the street, forcing him to wait until it had passed.

Most of the year the twins were preoccupied with football, not baseball. But since they'd finished their last football season at Hidden Valley—and the basketball season too, for that matter—baseball was the only game left in town from now until graduation.

By September their high school football careers would begin, and all thoughts of any other sport would vanish from their heads. But for now there was baseball—and tryouts for the team were this afternoon!

Tiki threw the ball up into the air, took a violent swing at it—and missed completely.

"Come on, 'Kirby'!" Ronde hooted. "If you want to get a candy bar named after you, like Reggie and the Babe, you've got to hit the ball!"

Tiki swung even harder this time. The ball went high and to the right. Ronde raced after it but had to pull back before hitting the front wall of the nearest house. The ball bounced off the porch roof with a loud *thunk*, and Ronde caught it before it hit the ground. "Yer out!" he cried happily, then took off running as the front door opened.

"Hey, you kids!" yelled the man who emerged. "Go play somewhere else! Get out of here before you break a window!"

"Sorry. Sorry," Tiki and Ronde both said. They *were* sorry too—but not as sorry as they'd been the day before, when each of them had broken a window with a badly placed fly ball. Repaying the neighbors would mean the boys would have to kiss most of their savings good-bye.

Still, that was the price of playing ball when there was no playground or park nearby. What were they supposed to do—stay home and watch TV all weekend?

Ronde came up to Tiki and handed him the ball, then took off his glove and stuffed it into his book bag. Tiki put the ball in his book bag, and the two of them sat there on the curb by the corner, waiting for the school bus to come by.

"You can hit pretty well," Ronde told him. "The problem is, you never know where it's going to go."

"So what?" Tiki shot back. "On a baseball field it doesn't matter, as long as it's fair."

"You think you can hit it out of the park at school?"

"I know I can," Tiki said. "Look how far I hit that second-to-last one just now."

"Yeah, but that was you playing fungo. What about with real pitching?"

Tiki shrugged. "How should I know? We've never played organized baseball. Never. Neither one of us. Not Little League, not in school, never."

"I know," Ronde said. "It's hard to get enough kids together to play a pickup game. Not like with football or basketball. You get four guys, you can play those sports."

"We had no real basketball experience either," Tiki said. "Still, even though we weren't the big stars on that team, we made a pretty big difference."

"I'm sure they're glad we joined the team," Ronde agreed. "I know I am."

"Me too."

The basketball team, which had been a complete mess before they'd joined it midseason, had finished up well, with a winning record, though not well enough to make the play-offs. It was the first team either of them had ever played on that hadn't made the play-offs, and it was a weird feeling for them. It made them both want to finish off their junior high school years on a high note.

"I think Coach Raines might have a pretty good team this year," Ronde said. "Especially if we're on it."

"Hey, we do have some baseball skills," Tiki went on. "It's not like we stink at it or anything."

"And we've watched plenty of games on TV," Ronde said. "So we know the rules and the strategies and stuff."

The twins fell into a long silence. Ronde broke it by saying, "You know, I'm a little scared about this tryout, actually."

Tiki gave a little laugh. "Me too," he said. "I think I can play, you know, but I have no proof. It's just in my head."

"Well, not totally," Ronde pointed out. "We're both pretty good at football."

"Yeah," Tiki agreed. "But who knows how today is going to work out?"

They'd decided to try out only last Friday. Before that they'd been figuring on keeping their jobs at Mr. Lanzberg's department store. But their mom had said, if they wanted to quit so they could play on the baseball team, it was okay. She was doing better at work now, she told them, and had gotten a raise at each of her jobs.

"The worst would be if one of us makes the team and the other doesn't," Ronde said.

"That would be bad," Tiki said, nodding.

"If you don't make it, I'm not gonna be on the team either."

"Why? I wouldn't be mad if you did. Not that it would ever happen. But if *I* made it and *you* didn't . . ."

"Don't even go there, yo," Ronde said. "That is not happening. I am not worrying about that one bit."

Tiki gave him a playful shove. "Quit flossin'," he said. "You *know* I'm better than you."

"Only at the plate. In the field I rule."

"You rule? You rule? Give me a break!"

Their playful back-and-forth was interrupted by the arrival of the school bus. They got on board and took their usual seats next to each other.

It was about a fifteen-minute ride, so Tiki settled in, putting his book bag on the floor between his feet and high-fiving the kids from the other stops as they filed past him on the way to their seats.

As the bus got rolling, Tiki sat back in his seat, his smile fading from his face. Ronde's words had troubled him. Even though Tiki had kept his doubts to himself, he too had been thinking about the prospect of them not making the team—or even worse, one twin making it and the other getting left off the squad.

Tiki remembered back in seventh grade, when they'd first tried out for the football team. They'd been nervous then, too, but not in the same way. After all, they'd had experience in Peewee Football League and already knew that they were good at the game.

As for the basketball team, that had been different too. It wasn't like they'd had to try out. They'd been asked to fill in midseason, when other players had left the team. It had been kind of a no-lose proposition: if they'd failed, well, no one would have blamed them. After all, they hadn't trained with the team. They'd been thrown into the fire, so to speak. On the other hand, if they'd played well, everyone would have been pleasantly surprised. Which was exactly how it had turned out.

By now everyone at Hidden Valley knew that the Barbers were the best athletes in their class—and probably in the whole school. Once people heard they were trying out, they would surely expect the twins to make the team. If that didn't happen—or if they made it and then stunk up the joint—it would be worse than embarrassing, Tiki thought. It would be downright humiliating!

The bus pulled to another stop, and their old friend Jason Rossini got on. Jason had been their quarterback in peewee league. He'd tried out for the football team back in seventh grade too—and when the coaches had listed him as third-string quarterback, he'd gotten insulted and quit.

Since then he'd emerged as a track star in the half mile. Sure enough, he was wearing his track jacket, the *HV* letters displayed prominently on the chest.

"Dudes!" he said, swinging himself into the seat across from them. "How goes it?"

"Good," Ronde said. "We're going out for the baseball team today."

"For real?" Jason shook his head and laughed. *"Why?"*

"What do you mean, why?" Tiki asked. "Why wouldn't we?"

"Cause baseball is for . . . Ah, never mind."

"No, say what you were going to say," Ronde told him. "Go on."

"Well, I was just saying, because, you know, why bother with a sport with nine guys on a side? Any one of them could mess up a game for you and turn a win into a loss. With track it's all about *you*. You win, you win. You lose, well, tough luck and do better next time. Think about it. With baseball, even if you win, the whole team gets the credit. In track, well . . . you get the picture. But, hey, suit yourselves. Who am I to tell you what to do?"

"Wait, wait," Tiki said. "Are you saying that when you were little, you sat in front of the TV and wished you could run the mile like what's-his-name?"

"Who?" Jason said.

"See, you can't even name the guy!" Tiki went on. "No, man, it was *baseball* you were watching. And football, and basketball. Those are the sports we dreamed about! Ronde and I, we're just going after our dreams."

Jason sighed and turned his palms upward. "Like I said, it's your call," he said. "But with the speed you two have got, it's a shame. You could tear it up in track, probably win a bunch of races. Get all the glory you deserve. . . ."

"Jase, it's not about the glory," Ronde said, shaking his head.

"Oh, no? Really? It's not?" Jason shot back. "Who are you kidding, dude?"

"No, you're the one who doesn't get it. It's about the *team*!" Tiki said. "Working together, standing or falling together!"

"He's right," Ronde agreed.

"Whatever. Forget I even said anything," Jason said, waving off the whole conversation. "Let me tell you, though, I was fourth in the state last year in the half mile, and I'm going to do even better this year. Maybe you don't think much of that, but I feel really good about it. And there'll be no teammates to screw me up with their mistakes. Just me against everyone else, plain and simple. It could be you guys too. You'd kill in the sprints, like I said."

Tiki was about to respond when Jason put a hand up to stop him. "I know. I know what you're going to say. Don't even bother; I get it. But if by some chance either of you doesn't make the baseball team—or if you do make it and live to regret it—remember there's always a spot for you on the track team. In fact, Coach Arkin said last year, 'Those Barber kids could run the hundred for me tomorrow.'"

Tiki squinted. "He actually said that?"

"Well . . . something like that. Something good about the two of you. I forget the exact words. Anyway, here we are."

The bus pulled to a stop in front of the school, and they all filed out. "Later," Jason said, waving good-bye and going up the steps to the front door of the building.

Tiki and Ronde watched him go. "Man," said Ronde. "He is a piece of work, isn't he?"

Tiki laughed. "Yeah. You've gotta say, though—he did do what he said he was going to do. He became a track star."

"Yeah. . . . Well, you ready?"

As they hitched up their book bags and headed for the door, Tiki kept hearing Jason's words in his head. That small, nagging seed of doubt kept growing inside him all day during his classes. Again and again he wondered if he and Ronde were doing the right thing by trying out for baseball.

2

TRIAL BY FIRE

"Mr. Barber? Are you with us? Or perhaps you're meditating on the fate of the universe?"

Ronde snapped to. "Uh, no, ma'am," he said, feeling the blood rush to his face as his classmates laughed at Mrs. Green's little joke at his expense. "I was just . . . um . . ."

"Yes, um indeed," said Mrs. Green with a smirk. "Would you like me to repeat the question?"

"Uh, yes, ma'am," Ronde said, which made everyone laugh again.

"Very well. The question was, who was the greatest philosopher of Athens during its golden age?"

History was usually one of Ronde's favorite subjects—even with Mrs. Green teaching it—but today his mind was on baseball tryouts, not ancient Greece. It was eighth period. In another five . . . no, four minutes the bell would ring, and Ronde would be on his way out to the field, where he always felt at home and fully alive. In the classroom it wasn't always that way—particularly if his mind was otherwise engaged.

"Um, Socrates?"

"That's right!" Mrs. Green said, surprised. She clapped for Ronde, which prompted everyone else in class to do the same.

Ronde heaved a huge sigh of relief when she went on to the next question and called upon the next innocent victim to answer. With some teachers nothing was ever fun. *Why was that?* he wondered.

The bell rang, mercifully, and Ronde felt his heart pounding with anxiety as he made his way downstairs and out the back doors to the playing fields behind the school. Several kids were already out there, throwing baseballs around or swinging bats to get warmed up. A lot of them looked really good—strong arms, soft hands with the glove, easy pivots at second base. . . . He nodded to himself, thinking that his competition looked pretty tough.

Ronde was surprised to find himself so nervous. He wondered if Tiki was feeling the same way, but he guessed that Tiki was—since the twins so often shared the same outlook about things. Looking around for him, he saw Tiki coming out the double steel doors, his glove already on his hand.

"Yo, yo!" he called out to Ronde.

Ronde waved, and tossed his book bag onto one of the bleachers. After fishing out his glove, he ran out onto the field, just in time to catch Tiki's toss. Soon the two brothers were warming each other up, playing catch, increasing the distance between them every few throws, waiting for things to begin.

After a few minutes they heard a shrill whistle. Ronde stopped midtoss and turned to see Coach Elliott Raines, his fingers in his mouth (that's what had made that ear-splitting sound!), an Eagles baseball cap on his head. Coach Raines also taught phys ed, and Ronde'd had him back in eighth grade. He was a tough, demanding teacher who was sure to be the same way as a coach.

"Okay!" Raines began, clapping his hands. "Everybody gather round!"

When all the kids were assembled—around fifty of them, it seemed to Ronde—the coach began his welcome speech. "Glad to see so many new faces this year. Of course, we've got about half of last year's guys coming back, so there are only a few slots available except for reserves. If you don't make the team, it doesn't mean you stink, okay? So don't let it get you down. It's just the reality of the situation.

Ronde looked over at Tiki, who returned his gaze with a worried look of his own.

"To start with," Raines went on, "I'm going to split

you kids into two groups. So start counting off!"

Ronde was number five, and Tiki number six. Ronde knew what that meant. When they separated odds and evens, he and Tiki would not be in the same group.

Sure enough, Ronde and the "odds" went out into the field to do drills with Mr. Barrett, the school guidance counselor and assistant coach, while Tiki followed Coach Raines as he led the "evens" to the batting cages for hitting tryouts.

If Ronde had felt nervous before, he was even more anxious without Tiki by his side. *This is crazy!* he told himself, trying to breathe deeply and slow his pounding heart. *I'm a good athlete. So is Tiki. We're gonna be okay. We're gonna make this team.*

A little voice in his head reminded him, *Not if you mess up.*

First Coach Barrett paired them off and watched them play long-toss. Ronde had a strong arm and could throw the ball a long way, but he had trouble controlling his throws. They went wild as often as not, out of reach of the kid who was supposed to catch them.

Not a good beginning, Ronde realized with a growing sense of dread.

Luckily, he did much better when it came to taking grounders, line drives, and pop-ups. Coach Barrett would hit the balls, fungo-style, to the two or three kids gathered at each position in the field. Each kid would take a turn fielding the ball, then give over to the next. After five or six rotations Coach Barrett switched the infielders with the outfielders.

Ronde aced these drills, even making one diving catch of a line drive that had the other kids saying, "Whoa!"

Next it was time for baserunning. Each kid did a circuit around the bases while Coach Barrett timed them with a stopwatch and wrote down their times in a ledger attached to a clipboard. Ronde clocked the fastest time in his whole group.

Still, they hadn't hit yet, and that was half the tryout. But before that happened, the hitting group came back from the cages. Now, with Coach Barrett pitching batting practice, Tiki's group got a chance to hit to Ronde's group as they took turns at their positions.

Ronde was anxious to see how his brother did at the plate, but in their bulky Eagle batting helmets, he couldn't tell one kid from the other.

That was probably because he was way out in center field, far, far away from the plate. Why had the coach stuck him way out here, along with a couple other kids who didn't look like they would make this team or any other? He sure hoped it didn't mean that the coaches were going to make him play the outfield—not before he had a chance to show them what he could do at short or second, or even on the mound!

Just as he was getting lost in these thoughts, the kid at

the plate launched a long, screaming fly ball in Ronde's general direction. Awakened by the crack of the bat, Ronde misjudged the ball at first, taking a step in before realizing it was going to be over his head. After reversing direction, he sped back toward the fence. Taking his eye off the ball just long enough to see where the fence was, he headed straight for the spot where he thought the ball would land.

It was almost out of his reach. But with one last lunge Ronde launched himself into the air, and felt his mitt touch the ball. With a quick flip of his mitt in midair, he shifted the ball from the edge of the glove into the pocket, where he squeezed it tight just an instant before he crashed to the ground.

Pain shot through his ribs and hip, but he held on to the ball, got up in one fluid motion, and fired it back to the infield, while everyone watching applauded and whooped in tribute to a truly great catch.

Ronde couldn't help smiling as the kid at the plate smacked his bat on home plate in frustration.

Then, on the very next pitch, the same batter cracked a line drive to Ronde's left. Ronde ran it down and snared it, ending his dive with a long slide across the slippery outfield grass.

As he held his glove up to show the ball, the batter slammed his bat on home plate again. Ronde could hear the boy's cry of frustration, but the kid, to his credit, didn't let it beat him. He smacked the next three pitches so far, even Ronde couldn't catch up to them!

As the other kids applauded, the kid at the plate took off his helmet and tossed it to the side. That's when Ronde realized exactly who had hit all those monster shots.

It was Tiki!

3

UPS AND DOWNS

Dang! Tiki said to himself as he high-fived the kids waiting for their turn at the plate. *Why didn't I think of playing baseball way back in seventh grade? I really like this!*

Truth was, he hadn't been expecting this level of instant success. But it had all been so easy. Somehow the baseballs the coach had thrown at him had seemed as big as grapefruits. He'd put everything he had into each swing, and hit the ball on the nose every time.

Tiki felt so good about his tryout so far, he wasn't even mad at Ronde for snaring two of his best shots. He was happy for his twin, who looked every bit like a starting center fielder out there.

Tiki was still half on a cloud when the two groups finally switched. It was time for his bunch to take the field.

He did fine on drills, showing good reaction time and soft hands on grounders in the infield, although some of the pop-ups did give him trouble. They were way up there, higher than any of the kids around Amherst Street had ever hit them. As he shielded his eyes from the bright sun, the first one hit the heel of his glove and bounced away. He had to duck out of the way of the second, just before it would have hit him in the noggin.

Whoa, he thought. *Getting hit with a baseball is much worse than a football!*

The near miss made Tiki a little gun-shy, which made tracking flies in the outfield even harder. The balls hit right at him confused him most—it was hard to tell at first if they were going to be long blasts or shallow pop-ups. This brief indecision made him break late, and miss one over his head, then another in front of him. Then he threw one in wildly on a deep fly, and missed the cutoff man he was supposed to throw it to.

And just like that, there went his good mood, and his high opinion of his own baseball skills.

Still, once they'd run the bases, he felt much better. Tiki posted the fastest time in his group, drawing oohs and aahs from the other kids, and meaningful, wide-eyed looks between the coaches.

Next it was time for Ronde's group to hit. Tiki watched for his twin and spotted him putting on his helmet. Stationed at second base, Tiki got down into his crouch.

"Come on, Bro," he said under his breath. "Hit it right here. Riiiight here," he repeated, smacking the pocket of his glove with his fist.

But Ronde didn't hit it to him. He didn't hit it much of anywhere. Although he was swinging for the fences, the farthest he got it was just past the mound. When his turn was done, Ronde took off his helmet and threw it to the ground.

"Hey! Hey! Respect for the equipment!" Tiki heard one of the coaches say. Ronde kicked the dirt on his way back to the bench.

Hmm, thought Tiki. It looked like he wasn't the only one named Barber having trouble at this tryout.

On their way home, taking the late bus, the twins had time to go over how things had gone for them. "I stunk up the joint," Ronde said.

"No, you did not! You made those great catches on me! Man, those would have been inside-the-park home runs!"

That got a smile out of Ronde. "Yeah, I kind of robbed you, didn't I?"

"No duh! *I* was the one who messed everything up."

"You? You hit it better than anybody, in your group or mine!"

And that made *Tiki* smile. "I did, didn't I? You know, I never felt that good at the plate before. . . . Course, it was only batting practice. He was throwing it so we could hit it."

"Dude, nobody else was creaming it like that. Batting practice or not, that was impressive."

"Yeah, I guess you're right," Tiki had to agree. He settled back into his seat and thought about it for a moment. "So, you think we made the team?"

"I hope so," Ronde said. "I *think* so, but . . ."

"I know. You never know, right?"

"Right."

"I mean, we weren't perfect, but neither was anybody else, right?"

"Right."

"Right. Man, I hope we make it," Tiki said.

"Me too. I feel like I've got baseball fever now."

"Ha! Me too, man."

"Yeah, spring is in the air," Ronde said, sighing.

The twins couldn't wait to get to school the next day. As soon as they entered the building, they ran to the big bulletin board in the entrance hall, looking for their names on the list of those who'd made the team.

"YES!" Ronde cried, pumping both fists in the air. "We're in, yo!"

"Where?"

"Right there!"

"Yeah, man! Give me five!"

They slapped hands so hard, they both said "OW!" and started laughing.

"Hey," said Ronde. "It doesn't say anybody's position. Just that we've got practice at three o'clock."

"Good with me. I brought my glove," said Tiki. "You?"

"Are you kidding? Of course I did!" Ronde said. "So, see you at three, Mr. T!"

The day flew by. Tiki barely noticed what was being discussed, and was lucky not to get called on by any of his teachers. He wouldn't have been ready to answer, no matter what the question was.

All he could think about was getting out on a field and playing a ball game—of any kind! It had hit him the night before that sports were so important to him right now in his life, nothing else mattered nearly as much.

He knew his mom would say that was a bad thing— that schoolwork had to come first. And he knew she was right. Still, that didn't change how he felt. He didn't know *how* to change that, and he wasn't sure he would, even if he could.

When the final period ended, Tiki raced down the hallways and stairs to the locker room, holding his book bag as if he were running downfield with the football, dodging anyone who got in his way. "Go, Tiki!" one kid yelled after him.

Half the team was already there when he arrived in

the locker room. Tiki recognized kids he'd known over the years. Many of them were ninth graders, like him. Tiki counted six kids who were no doubt returning as starters.

Nobody he was actually *friends* with, but that would come in time. When you played game after game with your teammates, it was like going to war together. Guys got closer, and friendships were formed in the heat of battle.

First they were issued uniforms. Tiki was lucky enough to get number four. "One of Rickey Henderson's numbers!" he told Ronde, who was holding up number three.

"That's me—Babe Ruth! He's got a candy bar too!"

"Yeah, that's you all right," Tiki said with a laugh. He didn't say the rest of what he was thinking. That maybe they should switch numbers, because Ronde's hitting was the opposite of Ruthian.

When they were all in uniform, one of the kids came over to Tiki and Ronde. "Hey," he said. "I think we had French class together," he said to Ronde. "Ian. Ian Lloyd."

They all shook hands. Then Ian told them, "You guys are gonna have to get baseball cleats. Those football cleats won't give you any traction on the dirt."

"Uh-oh," said Ronde. "How much do they cost?"

"Beats me," said Ian. "My mom takes care of all that stuff."

Tiki and Ronde exchanged glances. After Ian had shoved off to greet more teammates, Tiki said, "I guess there goes the rest of our savings, huh?"

"Definitely," Ronde said. "We can't ask mom to pay. It's gonna be at least fifty dollars."

"Man, that's a lot!" Tiki moaned. "But I guess it's worth it. We don't want to be sliding and slipping around on the infield."

Just then Coach Raines called the team to order. "Okay, gents," he began. "Listen up right here. First of all, welcome to the Eagles! Congratulations!" Everyone cheered and clapped. When the roar died down, the coach continued:

"I know this sounds crazy, but I don't make the schedules. Because of midterms and spring break, we got a late start on tryouts this year. The end result is that we've only just got a team together, and the season starts tomorrow."

A gasp went up from the assembled Eagles. *"Tomorrow?"* a few of them repeated in disbelief.

"I know, I know," said the coach, holding his hands up for quiet. "But every other team in the league's in the same boat, so no complaining. Let's just see how we do, and we'll make adjustments as needed.

"In the meantime I've drawn up a starting lineup and batting order based on what we saw at tryouts. At today's practice we'll work out at those positions. Bench players will hit to the starters, and field when they hit. So. Here's the list:

"Leading off, and playing short, Lenny Klein." Glancing over, Tiki saw that Ronde looked worried. Tiki thought he knew why too. He knew what Ronde thought—that the good players all got to play infield. And one of those positions was already gone.

"Batting second, in right field . . . Chris Jones. Batting third, playing third and relief pitching, Ian Lloyd."

Now it was Tiki's turn to frown. The first three hitters were usually the best, fastest kids on the team. Wasn't that him?

"Cleaning up, playing second, Tiki Barber."

A thrill went through Tiki, and he nearly leapt up and yelled "YESSS!" But he restrained himself. He knew it wouldn't look good, and more important, it would hurt Ronde's feelings.

But the cleanup spot! The single most powerful hitter on the team always hit fourth—and it was *him*!

"No pressure," Ronde said, grinning and offering him their personal, private handshake. Tiki grinned and accepted Ronde's congratulations. He knew how hard it was for his twin to put on a smile and give Tiki his props.

"Batting fifth, and playing left field, Michael Mason. Batting sixth, and catching, Cesar Ramirez. Batting seventh, playing first, Tyquan Brown . . ."

Now even Tiki was alarmed for his twin. He knew

Ronde had to be sweating blood, thinking he hadn't made the starting lineup at all!

Only two more slots to go—the last ones in the order. The weakest hitters in the lineup!

Well, Ronde didn't hit very well, thought Tiki. But he'd fielded well enough to start in center. He sure hoped the coach saw it the same way.

"Batting eighth, and pitching, John Benson. And in center field, batting ninth . . ."

Tiki held his breath. He saw that Ronde's eyes were shut tight, and his hands balled up into fists.

"Ronde Barber."

Tiki and Ronde exhaled together. Tiki quickly put an arm around his twin. "All right! The kid makes the starting nine!"

But Ronde didn't look happy. He looked away from Tiki, shaking his head. "Did he have to put me dead last?" he muttered, just loud enough for Tiki to overhear.

"Hey, you're not on the bench," Tiki pointed out. "You'll have lots of at bats to prove you belong higher up."

Ronde sighed. "I guess. Nothing I can do about it right now anyway."

"Okay, team," Coach Raines concluded, clapping his hands together. "Let's get out there and make the most of the little practice time we've got. Go, Eagles!"

"GO, EAGLES!" everyone shouted together, and they

crowded through the doors and out onto the field.

Ronde accompanied Tiki to second base. When they got there and Tiki stopped to take his position, he saw the look on his brother's face and knew that Ronde was feeling low. "Hey," he told Ronde, "center field is one of the most important positions on the team."

Ronde frowned, grunted, and turned away. He walked like a zombie the rest of the way out to center.

Tiki looked after him, worried. He knew that if Ronde didn't get over how he felt, it might affect the way he played. And that could snowball into a real disaster.

"Heads!" someone yelled, and Tiki snapped his attention back to baseball. He'd have to deal with Ronde later—if Ronde even *wanted* to be dealt with. Which wasn't very likely.

4

GAME ON!

Ronde could not get himself to sit still on the bus to North Side Junior High. "You've got ants in your pants!" Tiki complained, but it didn't make any difference.

Tiki, on the other hand, seemed calm and serious. *Well*, thought Ronde, *of course he's feeling good. He's playing second base and batting cleanup!* Whereas he, Ronde, was stuck out in center field, and batting dead last in the order. Not exactly a show of confidence in him by the coaching staff.

He had every reason to be nervous, he told himself. Already low man on the totem pole among the starters, he faced demotion to the bench if he messed up so much as even once!

These thoughts plagued him as he warmed up, long-tossing it with the other outfielders. A couple of times he misjudged a throw, and it went over his head. He sure hoped that didn't happen during the game.

As the visiting team the Eagles would be hitting first. Ronde sat on the bench and watched as his teammates immediately went to work on the Rockets' pitcher.

Lenny Klein, only five foot four inches tall, made a difficult target, and he didn't swing the bat unless the pitch was right down the middle. The previous season he'd been a standout in the field, and a pest on the bases as well. Picking up where he'd left off last year, Lenny wound up walking after a 3–1 count, and stole second on the first pitch to Chris Jones, who aside from the Barbers was the only new guy in the starting lineup.

Chris waggled his bat, then shot a hard grounder past the third baseman, but Lenny had to hold up at second to see if the ball went through. He wound up stopping at third, and the Eagles had runners at the corners.

Ian Lloyd was next up, but he was impatient. He swung at the first pitch, which was nearly over his head, and popped up weakly to the pitcher.

Tiki took one last swing in the on-deck circle and walked slowly to the batter's box, adjusting his helmet. Tapping his bat on the plate, and then pointing it at the pitcher, he looked dangerous, even from where Ronde was sitting.

"Hit it, Tiki!" he shouted. "Hit that ball!"

Tiki swung so hard, he nearly came out of his cleats.

"Strike one!" the umpire shouted. Tiki took the next pitch, right down the middle. "Strike two!" came the call.

"Come on, Tiki!" Ronde yelled. "This guy's got nothing!" It wasn't true—the pitcher was throwing very hard, and was just wild enough to put a scare into hitters.

Tiki stood his ground, pointed the bat at the pitcher again, and waited. The pitch was a changeup, and Tiki was fooled. Thinking fastball, he swung too soon, and hit only air. "Strike three!" the umpire said. "Yer out!"

Tiki slammed his bat on the dirt and walked slowly back to the bench. "That's okay, that's okay. We'll get 'em!" Coach Raines said, clapping his hands in encouragement. "Let's go, Mike!"

Michael Mason had hit the ball a mile in batting practice the previous day, and Ronde was hopeful he could do it here, too. Sure enough, with two balls and two strikes on him, he caught hold of one and sent it to deep center.

At first Ronde thought it would get past the center fielder. But the kid got a good jump on the ball and just managed to bring it in before he ran into the fence.

"Dang!" Ronde blurted out, disappointed that the Eagles had failed to score, despite getting their first two men on base. He grabbed his glove and headed onto the field.

He jammed his cap down low on his head and ran all the way out to center, determined that if a ball came his way, he would make a difference, just like the Rockets' center fielder had done.

Gone was his nervousness. Bouncing on the balls of his feet, Ronde stayed focused on the action taking place so far away from him. He clapped his mitt when John Benson struck out the first batter, and then the second.

Just as he was thinking he'd never see a ball hit his way all day, there was a loud crack of the bat, and suddenly it was heading straight at him!

No, no . . . it was going to go over his head! Ronde sprinted back toward the fence, keeping his eyes on the ball. At the last second he jumped onto the fence, reached up . . . and came down with the ball!

A groan went up from the Rockets and their fans, but the Eagles were ecstatic. "Attaboy, Ronde!" Coach Raines said, raising a triumphant fist and bumping Ronde's as he came back to the dugout.

The Eagles went down one, two, three in their half of the second inning. Then, in the bottom of the inning, Ronde watched helplessly as things started to shift in the Rockets' favor.

First their leadoff man got on base when his grounder went off John Benson's glove. Then Tiki fielded an easy double play grounder, but threw it too far to the right of second, and the shortstop couldn't make the grab.

It hurt Ronde to see his twin mess up such an easy play. Still, he had to admit he was glad it wasn't *him*. Coach wasn't going to sit Tiki on the bench unless he stopped hitting, and that wasn't likely to happen.

The Rockets managed to bring both runners home, for a 2–0 lead after two innings. Ronde grabbed a bat and prepared to lead off the top of the third. He came to the plate, suddenly feeling antsy again.

What if he struck out? What if the pitcher got wild and hit him with a pitch? What if . . .

The ball was coming! Seeing that it was going to be over the plate, Ronde lunged at it—and caught only air. "Stee-rike one!" came the call.

Ronde tried to slow his racing heartbeat. *Breathe*, he told himself. *You can do this.* He saw that the next pitch was high, and let it go by for ball one.

The next pitch was right at him, and he had to duck out of its way. "Ball two!" the umpire said.

Ronde swung through the next one and found it hard to believe he'd missed it. Truth was, he couldn't catch up to the speed of the fastball. If the pitcher had noticed and threw another just like it, Ronde was doomed.

But the kid threw a changeup instead, and Ronde let it go by as it dropped into the dirt.

Lucky for him. He couldn't have hit it if it had been a strike, because he was all geared up for the fastball.

Ronde felt like he was about to jump out of his skin. He was so wound up that if the next pitch had been any-where close, he would have leapt at it. But the ball was way outside, and Ronde took his base, blowing out all the tension when he got there.

Lenny Klein came up to the plate as the Eagles started chanting and cheering for a rally. Ronde saw this as his chance to impress the coach by using his speed. When Lenny worked the count to 3–0, Ronde took off for second on the next pitch.

Blood was pounding in his ears so loudly that he couldn't hear anything else. Nor did he look toward the plate to see what had happened on the pitch. As he approached second, he slid, just like Coach had shown them in practice.

But the ball was already in the second baseman's mitt, and he tagged Ronde out easily.

"What?" Ronde couldn't believe it. How had they managed to catch him stealing, with his speed?

Just as he sat back down on the bench, Lenny singled to left. *I would have got to third on that one,* Ronde realized. If only he had been more patient and given Lenny a chance to hit!

A quick glance at Coach Raines, who was shaking his head in frustration, showed Ronde that the coach was thinking the same thing.

They hadn't flashed him the *Steal* sign. He'd done it on his own. When the next two hitters struck out, the Eagles went down without scoring, and the score remained 2–0.

The Rockets did not score in the third. In the top of the fourth, Tiki started the inning by striking out for the

second time in the game. Ronde patted him on the back as his twin came back to the dugout, but Tiki shook him off. Ronde understood. Tiki was mad at himself for messing up, same as he was.

But that's when things started getting interesting. Michael Mason walked, and Cesar Ramirez singled. Tyquan Brown grounded out, but then John Benson came up and doubled both runners in to tie the score at 2–2!

Ronde came up with a chance to give the Eagles the lead—but he grounded weakly to first instead. Benson took third, and when Lenny and Chris both walked, it looked like the Eagles might break the game open. But Ian Lloyd grounded out to second, and the Eagles had to settle for two runs.

Oh well, thought Ronde. *At least we're not behind anymore.*

After Benson shut down the Rockets in the bottom of the fourth, Tiki led off the Eagle fifth by striking out again. Ronde could practically see the steam coming out of his twin's ears as he came back to the bench. Ronde knew better than to try and console Tiki when he was in this kind of mood. He turned back to watch the game, hoping that Tiki would put his frustration to good use, rather than letting it affect his play from here on out.

Michael Mason and Cesar Ramirez hit consecutive singles, and again, it looked like the Eagles were in business. John Benson walked, and the bases were loaded for Ronde.

He came to the plate, no longer thinking about how Tiki was doing, but only about himself. If he struck out, he would be totally humiliated! He tried to concentrate on just making contact . . . just making contact . . .

He made contact, all right. He hit the ball straight back to the pitcher—a soft line drive that turned into an inning-ending double play! Ronde felt like sinking into the ground, but instead, he fought back the urge, and grabbed his glove to head back onto the field. For a brief second, he and Tiki made eye contact, but each was too embarrassed to say a word to the other. They were stinking up the joint big-time, and they both knew it.

Come on! Ronde urged himself. *Get over it. It's not like we're losing—we're still all tied up. We could still win this thing!*

That was true—the game was tied, and it stayed that way till the bottom of the sixth. Then, as if in a bad dream, Ronde stood helpless in center field as the Rockets scored twice on a walk, followed by a big home run off Ian Lloyd, who had switched positions with John Benson after four innings and was pitching for the first time this year.

Ronde felt like he'd been dealt a crushing blow when that home run sailed over the fence, and he could see the rest of the team sag as well. Now it was 4–2, Rockets, and the Eagles were running out of at bats. The seventh inning was coming up, and in Junior High baseball, seven innings was all you got.

Ronde shook his head and set his jaw. *Hey, this game isn't over,* he told himself, *not by a long shot. We can still win it!*

Michael Mason led off with a long fly to left that was caught on the warning track. Again every Eagle player felt his hopes deflate like a balloon. Cesar Ramirez tapped back to the mound, and the Eagles were down to their final out.

But they weren't done yet. Tyquan Brown doubled down the right field line, and John Benson singled him in with his second hit of the day, to narrow the score to 4–3.

Now, amazingly, it all came down to Ronde.

He felt unsteady on his legs as he went to the plate. Staring at the ground, he tried to focus and pull himself together. So far today he'd swung at three pitches and whiffed on all three. If he struck out again now, he felt like he'd never live it down.

"Ball!" Ronde blew out a breath of air. That pitch had sure looked like a strike to him. He'd meant to swing at it but hadn't been able to pull the trigger in time, so he'd just let it go.

"Ball two!" cried the ump after a fastball whizzed over Ronde's head.

Ronde took a strike, then swung at another and missed. The count was 2–2, and now he and the Eagles were down to their final strike.

The next pitch was in the dirt, and John Benson took off for second. He had the base stolen before the catcher even threw the ball.

"Yeah!" Ronde shouted. "Yeah, baby!" He got back into the box, more determined than ever to deliver the tying run.

The ball was way outside. Ronde started to swing but somehow managed to pull his wrists back and let it go for ball four. "Yesss!" he said under his breath, grateful that he hadn't followed through.

Now the Eagles had the winning runs on first and second. Ronde watched as Lenny Klein came to the plate and looked to the third base coach to deliver the sign.

Ronde saw it. The coach touched the bill of his cap, then his right ear. That meant, *Take a pitch. Don't swing.* Then the coach turned to John and Ronde and touched his nose, then his left shoulder.

Steal! This time Ronde would be running on Coach's orders, and he made up his mind that no one was going to pick him off again, now or ever!

As soon as the pitcher went into his motion, Ronde was off and running. He saw John ahead of him headed for third. Ronde slid, his hands flying up to protect his head from the throw.

"Safe!" cried the second base umpire.

"Safe!" said the ump at third.

Ronde sprang up quickly. Looking toward third base,

he saw to his surprise that John Benson was about to head for home!

Ronde realized that the ball must have gotten away from the fielders, who were running after it frantically. Ronde took off immediately for third, and got there easily—only to find John Benson scrambling back toward him!

What was going on? he wondered. Why hadn't John scored?

Panicking, Ronde froze as the third base coach yelled something at him. "Back! Back!" he was saying, gesturing for Ronde to get off the bag at third.

And now he understood. John Benson had changed his mind about scoring when he'd seen the throw come home, and he'd turned back midway! If John got back to third while Ronde was still there, one of them would be called out, and the game would be over!

Ronde dashed back toward second base, but it was way too late. As soon as the catcher saw Ronde break, he threw back to second, and Ronde was caught in a rundown. The third base coach sent Benson back toward home, but Ronde was tagged out before Benson crossed the plate.

The game was over. The Eagles had lost.

And it was all his fault!

5

AFTER THE DISASTER

Amid the usual "We'll get 'em next time" and "They got lucky" pronouncements, there was a deep sense of letdown among the Eagles. It was a silence behind their brave words, and Tiki could hear it echoing in his own brain. What made it worse was that it had been largely his fault.

Well, no, that wasn't quite true, and he knew it. Ronde had made his share of mistakes too. None of the Eagles had hit very well off the strong Rocket pitching staff, and their pitching hadn't been great either.

Still, Tiki couldn't help feeling he and Ronde had let the rest of the guys down. Glancing over at Ronde, who was sitting beside him, staring into the pocket of his mitt, Tiki knew his twin was thinking similar painful thoughts.

Tiki remembered that other bus ride the week before,

sitting across from Jason Rossini. "In track when you win, it's all you," he'd said. "You don't have to share any of the credit. And if you lose? Well, at least it wasn't because someone else on your team messed up."

Maybe Jason was right, Tiki thought sadly. Maybe he and Ronde should have gone out for track. As much as the twins had stuck up for team sports, there was obviously a downside, too, and he and Ronde were feeling it now.

Tiki tried to find the bright side, the silver lining. "Well," he said out loud, "at least it was an away game. Our fans didn't have to see that mess with their own eyes."

"I hear you," Ronde agreed with a bitter laugh. "That was ugly."

"How ugly was it?" Tiki asked, the corner of his mouth turned up in the beginning of a smile.

"As ugly as a turtle wearing lipstick," Ronde said, starting to giggle.

"As ugly as moldy eggs on burnt toast!" Tiki replied.

"As a booger on a beauty queen!"

"As—"

And soon they were both laughing. The other kids couldn't help smiling as they tried to understand what was so funny. Pretty soon everyone was in on it, and the ride home was a game of How Ugly Was It?

As they all got off the bus in front of Hidden Valley

Junior High, waving good-bye as they headed for their rides, Tiki turned to Ronde and said, "Hey, you know what?"

"What?"

"It's funny, but I think maybe we just took the first step to becoming a team—and I don't mean the game."

Tiki stood at the plate, waggling his bat and waiting for the coach to throw him another one. He'd already belted the first pitch over the fence in left field and was seeing the ball like it was a big white grapefruit. The next pitch was low and in, but Tiki dropped the barrel of his bat and got there first. The sound of bat on ball was sweet and clean, and the ball soared into the sky, almost disappearing as he stared after it. It landed way, way over the fence, and everyone watching said, "Whoa!"

Parents sitting in the bleachers, kids doing baserunning drills, even people on the street walking by, all stopped what they were doing so they could maybe see another moon shot like the one they'd just witnessed.

After taking a couple pitches off the plate, Tiki whacked at a high fastball that had been right over the heart of the dish. He didn't miss it either. The ball took off like a rocket, a screaming line drive that made the center fielder freeze for an instant, before realizing it was going to be way over his head. He ran out of room at the fence, and the ball kept going. There was scattered applause as Tiki took off his batting helmet and headed back to the bench.

"Wow!" Coach Raines said, clapping him on the back. "Looks like you found something at the plate, huh?"

"I guess so," Tiki said modestly, even though inside he was bursting with pride and excitement. He couldn't wait for their next game!

It was a good thing that the Eagles' first game had been away from Hidden Valley, and from all the kids at school who had been his fans for the past three years. He hated to do badly in front of them, especially when most of them had never seen him play baseball before.

Tomorrow's contest against the Blue Ridge Bears, however, would be at Eagles Field. And after today's batting practice exhibition, word would surely get around fast. The stands were sure to be full for the team's home opener. Tiki could only hope he had half as much success tomorrow as he'd just had in batting practice.

For the game against Blue Ridge, Coach Raines had Tiki batting cleanup again. After all those home runs in batting practice, that came as no surprise to anyone. Ronde was batting ninth again—and was none too happy about it. Not that he had complained to anyone but Tiki—Ronde was too good a teammate to do that—but Tiki knew. He would have known even if Ronde hadn't said a word to him. Just by watching his twin, he could always tell what he was feeling. It was the easiest thing in the world for either of them to step inside the shoes of the other. That's what being an identical twin was all about, wasn't it?

Tiki felt Ronde's pain, but he also knew the coach was making a reasonable decision. Ronde was a light hitter at best and was having trouble catching up with fastballs. Until he learned to speed up his swing, he would have to get on base with his speed. That all added up to hitting ninth, at least for now.

The game started well for Hidden Valley. The Bears' hitters went down in order in the first. In the bottom of the inning, the pitcher had trouble finding the plate, walking the first two batters and hitting Ian Lloyd to load the bases with Eagles, with nobody out!

Tiki could hardly have picked a better situation. Brimming with confidence, he stepped to the plate, then took a couple of vicious cuts at the air to loosen up. He could hear the cheers of the Eagles fans who were packed into the bleachers. The beat of the bass drum accented their chants as he stepped into the box and waggled the bat high over his head.

The pitcher wound up. Tiki set his weight on his back foot, ready to launch another moon shot. Here came the pitch. Tiki swung so hard, he nearly came out of his shoes. But all he hit was air.

The cheers died down. As the catcher threw the ball back to the mound, Tiki tried to figure out how he'd missed that pitch. It had been right down the middle!

There wasn't much time to think, though. Here came the second pitch. Tiki, anxious to make up for missing, swung even harder—only to realize, too late, that the pitch was in the dirt. It got away from the catcher and Lenny Klein came halfway home from third before deciding it was too risky and heading back to his base.

The crowd started chanting again, bellowing with all their might. Tiki could feel himself sweating. One bead trickled down from his helmet, down his forehead, and onto his eyelid. He shook his head to get rid of it, just as the pitch came in.

He wanted to swing but held up, thinking the pitch was a little outside. By the time he realized it was curving back in toward the plate, it was too late. He watched it pass right over the heart of the plate, and heard the umpire yell, "Strike three! Yer out!"

A groan went up from the stands. Tiki wanted to smash something. Muttering under his breath, he returned to the bench, staring at the ground and ignoring the teammates who patted him on the back, saying, "Don't worry about it" and "We'll get 'em anyway."

The next batter, Michael Mason, hit the first pitch he saw right at the second baseman, who grabbed it out of the air, then tossed to first base, where Ian Lloyd had started heading for second. The double play ended the inning, as quickly as that.

Incredibly, after loading the bases with no one out, the Eagles had failed to score!

Demoralized and angry, Tiki grabbed his glove and headed out to second base. How had he missed that first pitch? Why had he even swung at the second? And how in the world had he let that third pitch go by?

He tried to get all these negative thoughts out of his head while he was in the field. Luckily, John Benson was pitching well, and the Bears weren't putting the bat on his fastball. If Tiki had to field a sharp grounder that inning, he wasn't sure he could have handled it.

After a scoreless second, Ronde walked to lead off the third. Good thing, Tiki thought. If his brother couldn't make contact, at least he could reach base by letting the pitcher walk him.

With Lenny Klein at the plate facing an 0–2 count, Ronde took off for second base. The pitch was in the dirt, but the Bears' catcher made the mistake of trying to throw Ronde out when it was way too late to get him. The throw bounced off Ronde's sneaker and into left field, and Ronde wasted no time in heading for third.

The left fielder threw the ball to home plate—but it got away from the catcher, and before anyone knew what was happening, Ronde was heading home! The catcher, stunned to see what was happening, fumbled at the ball as he tried to pick it up—and Ronde slid safely in with the first run of the game!

Tiki let out a whoop that was drowned in the sea of noise from all the Eagles and their fans. Ronde ran back to the bench, high-fiving everyone he could reach.

Unfortunately, that was all the scoring the Eagles did that inning. Nor did they even reach base in the next two innings. By the time the top of the seventh rolled around, the score was 3–2, Bears. John Benson had given up a big inning in the fifth, as his arm had tired and he'd started throwing the ball right down the middle instead of to the corners. The Eagles second run had come on a homer, with Michael Mason providing the heroics.

As for Tiki, he'd popped up twice to the infield, on swings that had been meant to produce home runs. He couldn't understand why it was happening—at batting practice the ball was right where he saw it. Today, though, he was swinging just over it, just under it, or was swinging too soon or too late. He wasn't off by much, but that little bit was the difference.

As he was dwelling on all this, the Bears' cleanup hitter smacked a hard ground ball to his right. He dove for it, and came up with it in his mitt. Springing to his feet, he fired the ball toward first—but his aim was way off. He'd rushed the throw, not realizing that the hitter was a slow runner and Tiki had plenty of time. The throw sailed wide of first, rolling straight under the fence and into the stands.

The umpire signaled that the hitter was to take third

base on the unplayable ball. Tiki hung his head and kicked the dirt with his toe.

Just what they needed! It was one thing for a team to come back in the last at bat from being down one run. But if the Bears scored this insurance run, it would be that much harder. And it would all be his fault!

Sure enough, two strikeouts later, a base hit scored the run, making it 4–2, Bears.

In the bottom of the seventh, Tiki had one last chance to make things right. As Tiki was walking to the plate as the winning run, with men on first and second and two outs, Coach Raines cautioned him to "Just go for a base hit! A base hit ties the game!"

Tiki heard the words, and he understood their meaning. But in his head a voice kept telling him, *One swing of the bat wins this game! One big home run! You can do it, dude!*

Tiki took a strike, wanting to get a feel for the Bears' relief pitcher's stuff. He wasn't throwing as hard as the first guy. Tiki thought he could see the ball well coming out of the kid's hand. He reared back and swung, ferociously.

"Strike two!" yelled the umpire as the ball landed in the catcher's mitt.

Tiki nearly fell to the ground, so hard had he swung. His whole body had twisted like a pretzel, and he'd lost his balance.

The next pitch was high and inside. Tiki ducked, but the ball hit his bat and went foul. "Strike two!" the umpire called.

Tiki was really sweating now. He had to keep shaking his head to keep the salty, stinging drops out of his eyes.

The pitch came in fast. Tiki took one last, explosive, salt-blinded swing at it—and missed!

"Strike three! Yer out! Ball game over!" the umpire yelled.

Tiki heard him, even over the loud moan that came from the stands and the Eagles bench. Another Eagles loss!

And this time everyone would be pointing the finger straight at him.

To his surprise, in the locker room nobody said a mean word. Those who came up to him patted him consolingly on the back and muttered words of consolation and encouragement.

But it didn't help. Tiki knew the truth—all he had to do was look at Ronde to confirm it. Ronde, who'd struck out twice after his early heroics, but whom nobody had been counting on for his bat, couldn't even look him in the eye.

Even Ronde knows this loss was on me, Tiki thought. *I've got to get myself turned around somehow—and fast!*

6

HARD TIMES

The Eagles were 0–2 out of the gate, and Ronde was feeling totally bummed out. He was so upset, he was barely able to focus on his schoolwork. In fact, Ms. Bernstein, his English teacher, had called him over after class and asked him if there was some trouble at home she should know about.

He'd told her there wasn't—which was true—but didn't mention his worries about what was happening to him at the plate. He knew she wouldn't understand. Ms. Bernstein had more than once mentioned that she thought playing sports in junior high school was a waste of time—time that would be better spent studying or doing homework.

Ronde knew his mom would agree about the studying part, and he promised Ms. B. that he would pay better attention from now on. But he also knew that until and unless he solved the mystery of his total failure in the batter's box, he would be distracted by feelings of defeat, misery, and frustration.

That afternoon at practice he hit okay, as he sometimes did in practice. That got him to wondering why in real games he whiffed nine swings out of ten. It couldn't just be a coincidence, he realized.

His problem had to be with the speed of the pitches. Coaches at batting practice wanted you to make contact, so they threw the ball right down the middle, at a speed any batter could catch up to. In game action the other side's pitchers were trying to make you *miss*. They would throw balls that looked like strikes, and strikes that looked like balls—and before you knew it, you were confused and swinging at thin air.

Ronde thought his problem was that he would get used to the speed of batting practice pitches, then be consistently behind when it really counted. He made a decision to try a drastic remedy—after all, if there ever were a time for desperate measures, this was it.

He decided that he was going to cheat.

That is, whenever he thought the next pitch was likely to be a fastball, he would start his swing early, before he even knew how fast the pitch was or where it was going to be. He might miss badly if it turned out to be a changeup or a curveball. But it was his only chance of catching up to a good fastball. And so far fastballs had accounted for about two out of every three pitches he'd seen.

Ronde figured that if he started hitting those fastballs, word would get around the league eventually, and pitchers would start throwing him pitches he could actually catch up to with his normal swing.

He knew this decision was a big gamble, but he figured he didn't have much to lose. He hadn't gotten a hit in either of the first two games—hadn't hit the ball fair even once! Just strikeouts and the occasional lucky walk.

Convinced that whatever happened would at least be different from what he'd done before, Ronde readied himself to face the Martinsville Colts. It was another home game for the Eagles, so whatever happened, it would all play out in front of hundreds of his friends, teachers, and schoolmates.

As he took the field for the start of the game, Ronde saw Jason Rossini on the adjacent running track, practicing for his next meet. Jason waved to Ronde, and gave him two thumbs-up. Ronde waved back, thinking as he did so that maybe he should have gone out for track, like Jason had suggested.

Ronde hated the thought that the last memory Hidden Valley's students and teachers would have of him might not be as a football hero but as a baseball failure.

He didn't have much time to think about it, fortunately. On the first pitch of the game, Martinsville's leadoff man cracked a line drive to center field. Ronde stood frozen in place at first, trying to gauge how hard the ball had been hit. It seemed to rise in midair, gaining extra speed as it went. Ronde took off toward the wall, taking his eye off the ball for a second to see how much room he had to roam.

As he approached the chain-link fence, Ronde leapt into the air, extended his arm, and grabbed the screaming liner out of the air. He crashed into the fence, protecting himself with both arms up. When he came down, he stumbled, then held up the glove to show that it contained the ball. A roar went up from the stands, and Ronde forgot all about his hitting troubles—at least until the bottom of the second, when he came up to the plate for the first time.

By then the Eagles led, 2–0, on a towering home run by Tiki, who'd connected on the Colts' pitcher's tempting change-up and crushed it, scoring Lenny Klein from second base, where he'd arrived after a leadoff double.

Ronde tapped the plate with his bat, measuring his distance from it in the batter's box. He dug his cleats into the soft dirt, trying to get good footing. It hadn't rained in three weeks, and the ground was dusty and soft. He held his bat back way behind his shoulder, wound like a spring ready to uncoil.

There was one out, and a man on first due to a walk by the Colts' pitcher. Ronde knew that a speedy runner like John Benson was likely to steal. He was already taking a big lead off first, and the pitcher could see that, too—which meant he'd want to stick to fastballs, giving his catcher a chance to throw out the runner at second.

As the pitcher went into his windup, Ronde reared back as far as he could. He went into his swing a split second earlier than he otherwise would have—and amazingly, was rewarded with solid contact!

The ball bounced twice down the third base line and hit the bag before the third baseman could glove it. The ball ricocheted high into the air, and by the time the Colts had retrieved it, Ronde was on second base and Benson was standing on third!

"Attaboy, Ronde! Attaboy!" Ronde heard Coach Raines yell. Ronde clapped his hands together and crammed his helmet back onto his head. He took his lead, hoping Lenny would drive him and John in for two more runs.

But Lenny only flied to left. John Benson scored the Eagles' third run on the sac fly, but Ronde had to stay at second while the throw went to third. Chris Jones and Ian Lloyd both walked to load the bases—but Tiki struck out to end the inning, stranding all three runners.

The Colts scored twice in the top of the fourth and were threatening to tie the score. With one out, men on second and third, and their cleanup man at the plate, Ronde backed up to make sure nothing would be hit past him.

With a full count the hitter popped one up to shallow

center! Ronde's eyes went wide as he realized he could never reach it because he was playing so deep.

Or could he? Ronde took off like lightning, running for all he was worth. The ball was falling now, dropping almost straight down. He figured the runners would both be going, assuming the ball was going to drop in for a hit—but he couldn't take his eyes off the ball to look.

At the last second Ronde launched himself forward, reaching so hard he thought his arm would detach itself from the rest of his body—and caught the ball only inches from the ground!

He hit hard, doing something of a face-plant in the grass. But he made sure to squeeze his mitt tight. Coming up in one swift motion, he fired the ball to second base, where Tiki was waiting for it. The runner had no chance of getting back in time, and a would-be disaster was transformed into an inning-ending, Barber-to-Barber double play!

Still with the lead, the Eagles were determined to extend it and secure their first victory of the season. Tiki, who had struck out in the second, did it again in the bottom of the fifth.

Then, with two out and nobody on in the bottom of the sixth, Ronde managed to pull another fastball between the third baseman and the bag. Soon after, he stole second, and then third base!

Lenny followed by drawing a walk, but Ronde was

stranded at third when Chris popped up to the pitcher, and the score remained 3–2, Eagles. That one run lead felt very, very shaky to a team that had done nothing yet but lose.

In their half of the seventh, facing defeat, the Colts finally broke through and tied the game. Ronde slammed his mitt to the ground out in center when he realized the Eagles might not get their first win after all. But he quickly picked the glove up again and got himself ready for the next hitter.

The bases were loaded, and Ronde could only watch in frustration as Ian Lloyd, tiring after pitching five innings for the first time, walked the next three hitters to put Martinsville ahead, 6–3.

The Eagles entered the bottom of the seventh facing a third straight loss to start their season. But they still had three outs to work with, and right away they showed they would not go down without a fight.

Ian Lloyd began the inning with a double, somewhat making up for his wildness on the mound, but Tiki followed that by striking out for the third time in a row!

Luckily, the Colts' reliever, who had been throwing a lot of pitches himself, chose just that time to lose the plate. He walked the next two hitters, then hit Tyquan Brown to bring in a run, still with only one out!

The score was now 6–4, and the Eagles had life. Unfortunately, they were coming to the bottom of their batting order—their weakest hitters—just when they needed a hit most.

The number eight man, John Benson, who had shifted from pitching to third base after the first four innings, hit a sharp single to center, scoring Michael Mason from third, and giving the Eagles their fifth run of the game, still with only one out.

The stands erupted in cheers and the thumping of drums. Now it was up to Ronde. A walk would tie the game. A hit would almost surely win it.

Ronde was ready for the fastest fastball, and was so wound up that he swung at the first pitch, even though it was in the dirt.

"Stee-rike one!" the umpire bellowed.

"Stay loose, Ronde!" Coach Raines called out to him from the bench. "Breathe!"

Ronde lunged at the next pitch, a curve, and was way ahead of it. "Stee-rike two!" the umpire yelled.

Ronde told himself to relax. He breathed deeply, remembering the coach's words. When the pitch came, he swung early, and hard—and hit a slow grounder to short.

Ronde ran like the wind as the shortstop threw to second for one out. The second baseman fired the ball to first—but Ronde was too fast, and he beat the throw by a whisker. "Safe!" called the ump, as Cesar crossed the home plate with the tying run!

The crowd and the Eagles' players all erupted in wild

cheering. But the cheering quieted down again when Lenny grounded out to end the inning with the game still tied, 6–6.

The game went on, into extra innings. With Benson and Lloyd both already used as pitchers, Coach Raines called Tiki in from second base to pitch!

Tiki looked stunned when he was handed the ball, but Ronde saw him nod as the coach gave him a quick pep talk.

Amazingly, even though he walked three batters and threw a ton of pitches, Tiki got through the inning without giving up a run. *Whew!* thought Ronde, trotting in from the outfield. *Let's hope we don't need Tiki to get us another three outs!*

In the bottom of the inning, the first two Eagles hitters grounded out. Then everyone leaned forward as Tiki came to the plate. In spite of his three strikeouts, they all knew he had the power to end this game with one swing. He'd homered in the first inning, so why not again now?

With two out and no one on, Tiki was swinging for the fences all the way. But instead of making solid contact, he wound up hitting a dribbler right in front of the plate!

Everyone was so shocked that for an instant no one moved. Tiki was the first to kick his motor into gear, and with lightning speed he streaked toward first base. The catcher and pitcher both went for the ball, but it was exactly halfway between them, and neither of them came up with it cleanly. Tiki reached first safely, on the weakest hit anyone had had all day!

On the first pitch to the next batter, Tiki was off to steal second. The catcher threw, but the ball bounced into center, and Tiki got up and kept right on going! By the time the throw came in to third, he was on his way home—and the throw there arrived at the same time he did. . . .

"Safe!" the umpire called.

And it was over. Just like that. The Eagles had won their first game, 6–5, in the most unpredictable of ways!

All his teammates mobbed Tiki, and the happy mood continued long afterward in the locker room as the players showered and changed.

Tiki and Ronde were right in the middle of it, enjoying their hard-won victory like everybody else, when Coach Raines's voice caught them up short.

"Tiki! Ronde!" he called. "Don't go anywhere. I need to speak to you both—privately."

Uh-oh, Ronde thought. *What's this all about?* He looked over at Tiki, but his brother was obviously just as in the dark as he was.

One thing was clear, though. From the tone of the coach's voice, this could not be good.

7

A CHANGE IN THE ORDER

"One at a time," Coach Raines told the twins.
Pointing to Ronde, he said, "You first. Follow me." With
a glance back at his brother, Ronde followed the coach
down the little hallway to his office. Ronde looked like
he was going to the electric chair.

"This might take a few minutes," Coach Raines told
Tiki as he held the door open for Ronde. "You might
want to crack a book open or something while you're
waiting. Never hurts to get some studying done."

As soon as the office door closed, Tiki got up and left
the locker room. He couldn't concentrate on schoolwork—
not right now. There was something else he needed to do
right away, before even talking to the coach.

For the past two games Tiki had been constantly
wondering what was wrong with his game. Finally, after
striking out three times in a row today, it dawned on him

there might be something wrong with *him*. More specifically, with his *eyesight*.

Tiki headed quickly down the hall to the nurse's office and opened the door. No one inside at the moment—a good thing as far as Tiki was concerned.

Spotting the eye chart on the far wall, he stood on the red line and covered his left eye. Thankfully, his right eye could read even the smallest line of text just fine. Covering his right eye, he saw that there was nothing wrong with the left one either.

"Tiki? Are you okay?" The nurse was just coming into the office.

Tiki whipped his hand away from his eye. "Oh. Yeah. Fine. I was just . . . going," he said, and slipped past her before she could think what in the world he could be doing there if he wasn't sick.

Tiki ran back down the hall to the locker room, and saw that the office door was still closed. Inside he could hear Coach Raines's voice. He wasn't shouting, but he didn't sound happy, either. Tiki forced himself not to listen.

He should have been relieved to find out that there was nothing wrong with his eyesight. But strangely, he felt worse, not better. If the problem wasn't that he needed glasses, what was it? What was causing him to choke in big situations, game after game?

The door opened, and Ronde came shuffling out. He did not meet Tiki's gaze but instead just sat down next to him on the bench. "Your turn," he said. "I'll wait for you here."

Tiki glanced up at the open door, then back at Ronde. He wanted to ask his twin what the coach had said, but something in Ronde's manner stopped him. Instead he rose slowly and trudged into the office.

"Take a seat, Tiki," said Coach Raines, who was seated behind his desk, looking at a bunch of scorecards. When Tiki was seated, the coach continued. "I'm looking here at your at bats," he said, shuffling the papers around. "Two for thirteen, a bunch of strikeouts, one home run, one infield hit. Overall, I'm not happy, and you shouldn't be either."

"I'm not!" Tiki said sincerely. "I just don't know what to do about it, though. I'm seeing the ball okay—I checked and my eyes are twenty-twenty!"

"Hey, it's okay," Raines said, holding up a hand and offering Tiki a quick smile. "I believe you, kid. It's just, something's gotta change here. We're 1–2, and we could have easily gone 0–3 just now."

Tiki had to fight back the lump that was rising in his throat. It sure sounded like the coach was blaming him and Ronde. Why hadn't he called on anyone else to stay? It was the only reason Tiki could think of.

"Look, I'll level with you, Tiki. You and your brother are the best athletes we've got. You've both got speed, and good gloves, strong arms, and *you*'ve got some nice pop in your bat besides."

Tiki was taken aback by the coach's words. He'd expected to get chewed out. "Uh, thanks," he managed to say.

But Coach Raines wasn't finished. "If our team is going to make a good showing this year, it's got to be you and Ronde leading the way. Some nice baserunning, a lot of excellent fielding, but too many mental errors. And that's why neither one of you is hitting a lick."

Tiki felt smacked down again. Hadn't the coach just been praising him and Ronde?

"Ronde's got some issues with his swing, but in your case I think it's all about your approach at the plate. The good news is, I think I know how to help you."

"O . . . kay . . ."

"Here's the problem—you're trying to hit a home run every single pitch."

"Yeah? So?" Tiki was confused. Wasn't that the cleanup hitter's job?

"In a way it's my fault," the coach said. "I probably shouldn't have batted you fourth. But from now on you're going to be hitting leadoff."

"What?" Tiki bounded up out of his chair, but the coach stood up, reached over the desk, put a hand on his shoulder, and gently sat him back down.

Tiki felt the sting of hurt pride. The coach was demoting him, that was what it felt like.

"I've been considering it for a while," Coach Raines

explained. "I want you and Ronde to concentrate on just getting on base. With your speed it messes up the opposing pitcher's rhythm. I've seen what happens when you're out on the base paths. Trouble is, neither one of you is getting on enough. In your case it's because you're always in home run mode. You've got to start hitting to the situation more."

"Huh?"

"How many outs are there? Who's on base? Are they fast? What's the score? What inning is it?"

"Yeah . . . ?" *No, duh*, Tiki thought. *Like I don't know that already.* But he knew there was some truth in what the coach was saying. He'd been thinking about all the home runs he hit in batting practice, not the game situation at that moment.

"You've got great power," the coach said, "but when you swing for the fences, your swing is totally out of control. Like this." Stepping back to make sure he had enough room, Coach Raines proceeded to demonstrate a wild home run swing. "I think you even closed your eyes that last at bat, didn't you?

"It's okay if you hit a single," said the coach, putting the bat back down. "Especially if it drives in a run. And it's okay to take a pitch if it's not in the right place."

"Huh?"

"For instance, you've got a man on first with nobody out. You want to hit it to the right side of the infield, between first and second—because that advances the runner, even if you ground out. And another thing—I told your brother this too—don't always be trying to pull the ball. Hit the ball where it's pitched. If it's outside, go the other way with it—hit it to left field."

"But you just said to hit it to the right side!" Tiki said, confused.

"See, that's exactly what I mean! It depends on the situation."

Tiki sighed. "Okay, Coach. I get it, I guess. So, can I still bat cleanup if I change my approach?"

"You're my leadoff man from now on, Tiki. Start thinking like one. All you've got to do is get yourself on base and start causing havoc with your speed. Next practice I want you to focus on baserunning drills. And in batting practice try to hit ground balls so you can use your speed to leg out hits. Practice your bunting, too. And don't forget—when it comes to game time, a walk's as good as a hit, so don't even think about swinging at pitches that aren't strikes.

"Cheer up, kid. It's not the end of the world, and it's going to make us a better team. Remember, Tiki—we're gonna win as a team, with everybody contributing, or we're not gonna win at all."

That hit Tiki right where he lived. He'd always prided himself on being all about the team! Hadn't he told Jason that when they'd been comparing baseball to track?

"And besides," Coach Raines added with a wink, "hitting leadoff, you might get an extra at bat every game. The more times you come to the plate, the happier I'll be." He laughed, and added, "You'll probably wind up hitting more homers this way, anyway." He got up and opened the door for Tiki.

"Okay, that's all. See you at practice."

Ronde rose as Tiki approached, and both boys, without a word to each other, shuffled out of the locker room and headed home.

The weather had turned warmer, and the days had gotten long enough now so that they could bike to and from school. As they rode, Tiki and Ronde both remained deep in thought.

Tiki had no problem admitting he wasn't perfect. Still, it was hard to hear it from your coach. Worse, Coach Raines had asked to see them in front of everyone. If Tiki or Ronde came into practice tomorrow with a long face, everyone would know they'd been chewed out.

He couldn't get over it—in his whole athletic career, this was the first time he'd ever gotten a "talking to" by any coach. It still stung, but Tiki was a team player at heart, and he knew he needed to use criticism to improve, not to get more negative in his thinking.

Besides, he had to admit that what he'd been trying so far hadn't been working. In spite of all the homers he'd hit in practice, he'd had only one that counted in a game. Aside from that he'd gotten only on base one other time.

"We need to take charge of this team winning," he finally said out loud.

Ronde looked over at him. The two were riding side by side now, on the empty side streets of their neighborhood. "He tell you to just get on base too?"

"Uh-huh."

"We're gonna do it, right?"

"Uh-huh. I'm gonna make it my business to get on base every time."

"Me too."

"Gimme five!"

They reached out and slapped five, their bikes wobbling until they regained control. "Last one home's a rotten egg!" Ronde shouted, and they were off and riding, feeling better again.

A NEW APPROACH

Two days later the news was all over the school.
Jason Rossini had won the half mile race in the big track
meet against archrival Pulaski and was in position to
compete for the state title. Everyone was talking about
the school's newest sports hero—Jason—and Ronde,
while he was happy for his old friend, still felt a tug in
his gut that it wasn't him or Tiki being celebrated.

The twins had gotten used to being sports heroes at
Hidden Valley. At the end of June they would be gone.
Would anyone even remember them next September?

Here came Jason down the hall, with his books under
one arm and a gigantic trophy under the other. His grin
stretched from ear to ear, and he laughed as one kid after
another patted him on the back and congratulated him.

Ronde, too, joined the line of kids paying tribute.
"Good going, dude," he told Jason.

"Thanks," Jason replied with a one-sided grin. "Bet you're sorry now you didn't sign up for track, huh?" It wasn't even really a question.

Ronde sighed. "You know, we're gonna be okay. I'll bet you right now we finish with a winning record."

"Taken," Jason agreed, shaking pinkies with Ronde to seal the bet. "Anyhow, who cares? What's a winning record mean—you don't even necessarily make the play-offs. Even if you did, what are your odds of ending up with one of these?" He held up his trophy for effect, but he needn't have bothered. Ronde knew exactly where he was coming from.

"Later, man," he told Jason, and headed for practice with a big chip on his shoulder.

Ronde was as determined to lift his team to a winning season as he'd ever been about anything. Even if just to show Jason that it wasn't all about individual glory. Sometimes it was all about the team and your contribution to it. That was something Jason couldn't understand, and nothing Ronde could say to him was going to change that.

"Hey, it's still not too late!" Jason called after him. "You two could probably edge out some of our weaker sprinters!"

Ronde shook his head as he kept walking. He wasn't about to show up and take some kid's place who'd worked hard all year at improving. How would that kid feel, getting shoved aside midseason for a pair of newbies? Besides, even if he and Tiki were faster than the kids they replaced, neither of them would have felt right about it.

Ronde suddenly realized that, just by thinking so hard about it, he was actually considering Jason's suggestion. *Well, that's okay*, he figured. It was okay to imagine every possibility that came along in life, so long as he stood by his basic principles in the end.

No, he would stay on the baseball team and make it work. He thought back to what Coach Raines had told him the other day. He'd told Ronde that he'd been helping the team in the field and on the bases but hurting them at the plate.

Coach had told him to be more selective about which pitches he swung at, especially with fewer than two strikes. "Go for pitches down in the zone," he'd said, "so you can hit the ball on the ground. Even if an infielder gets to it, half the time you're going to beat it out for a hit. If you hit it in the air, even if you hit it as far as you can, it's not leaving the park, understand? Your odds of getting on base go way down."

Coach had also told him to stop trying to pull everything. "Especially outside pitches, because if you try to pull them, you'll just roll over the ball and hit a dribbler. Better to swing less hard, go to the opposite field. You're much more likely to make solid contact that way." Last but not least, Coach had told him to learn how to bunt.

• • •

At practice Ronde noticed that Coach Raines gave both him and Tiki extra swings in the batting cage. He saw that Tiki was practicing the same sorts of things the coach had prescribed for Ronde. Bunting, going the other way, hitting the ball on the ground, laying off bad pitches.

Ronde wondered where the home runs would come from. If Tiki wasn't hitting homers for them, who would?

But he'd been on enough teams to know that because coaches saw everything that was going on, they usually knew best.

Taking his turn in the cage, it felt strange to see the ball coming toward him and not trying to hit it as hard as he could. He found himself swinging late, or waving at pitches. The longer he hit, the more confused he got. Even bunting, he found himself stabbing at the ball instead of "catching it" with the bat.

As the twins rode home afterward, Ronde was even quieter than usual. All he could think about was Jason Rossini and what he'd said.

Maybe he was right, Ronde thought. *Maybe I should quit this game and go out for track. . . .*

Even though it was midseason, even though he'd be costing some other kid a spot, what was the use of staying on the baseball team and failing miserably game after game after game?

• • •

The East Side Mountaineers were 3–0 so far and were the Eagles' stiffest challenge yet. They had a pitcher who was six feet tall and threw the ball faster than anyone else in the league. Kids who had been on the team the year before said he was wild, too. You had to be ready to duck at any time.

Great, thought Ronde. *Just what I need.*

He watched as Tiki stepped up to the plate to start the game. Tiki watched one pitch go by for a strike.

Ronde hadn't even been able to see the ball! He wondered how Tiki, or any of them, were ever going to get on base against this pitcher.

But then Tiki found the answer. On the second pitch he squared to bunt, and laid a beauty down the third base line. He made it to first without even a throw! Ronde glanced over at Coach Raines, who was clapping hard and giving Tiki the thumbs-up sign.

With Lenny Klein at the plate, Tiki took off for second. The pitch was in the dirt, and when Tiki got up, he saw that the catcher hadn't caught up to the ball—so he took off for third!

The throw there was high, and the third baseman leapt to catch it but couldn't come down with the ball. By the time he retrieved it, Tiki was crossing home plate with the game's first run!

"That's how we do it!" Coach Raines hollered. "Attaboy, Tiki!"

The next three Eagles hitters went down without even making contact, but it didn't matter. For now they still had the lead—if only they could keep it.

Tiki fielded two sharp grounders for the first two outs of the next half inning. Then a screaming liner came Ronde's way. He reached for it, and the ball went off the end of his glove and landed a few feet away. He ran to get it and, seeing that the hitter was heading for second, threw a bullet to the bag that nailed the runner midslide!

"Yeah! Yeah! Yeah!" Coach Raines bellowed. "That's keeping your head in the game! Great play!" He was more excited than Ronde had ever seen him!

Ronde came to bat in the second inning with two men on and two down. He knew enough not to try to bunt with two outs, and a ground ball would mean a force at any base but home. So he knew the coach's advice didn't apply to this situation. He either had to walk and leave it up to Tiki, who was on deck, or somehow get a ball through the infield and drive in the runs himself.

The first pitch whizzed by his ear, and Ronde threw himself to the ground to avoid it. The second pitch froze him as it dropped over the plate—a changeup!

Wasn't this guy's fastball hard enough to hit? He had to have a changeup, too?

Ronde saw another changeup coming and lunged at it, but he was too quick and the ball plopped into the catcher's mitt for strike two.

Now he had to protect the plate, he knew. The fast-ball screamed toward his head, and he ducked again—but it wasn't a fastball after all. It was a curve, and it dropped across the plate while Ronde cowered with his hand across his face.

"Stee-rike three! Yer out!" the umpire called.

Ronde, more frustrated than ever, headed back to the bench and grabbed his mitt. Next time up, he swore to himself, he'd be ready to swing at any pitch that was close.

John Benson, the Eagles' pitcher, settled into a good groove and kept the Mountaineers scoreless for the next two innings. Meanwhile Tiki bunted his way on for a second straight time—and this time Ian Lloyd, the new cleanup man, hit a double to drive him in for the second Eagles run.

Ronde got another chance at the plate in the top of the fourth, with a man on third and two out. This time he swung blindly at two straight pitches, hitting nothing but air. On the third pitch he took a ball in the dirt. The man on third almost came home but thought better of it, and a good thing too. The catcher retrieved the ball and would have had him dead to rights.

The next pitch looked inviting to Ronde, and he swung at it, trying only to make contact. But he'd mis-read the pitch. It was a changeup not a fastball, and Ronde was way ahead of it.

"Stee-rike three!" the ump yelled, and once again Ronde went back to the bench, defeated. "I stink at this game!" he muttered to himself as he grabbed his mitt.

In the bottom of the fourth, East Side came back to score two runs and tie it up. But in the fifth, Tiki got an infield hit leading off. He stole second, and came home with two outs on an error by the Mountaineers' first baseman, as the Eagles regained the lead, 3–2.

The score stayed that way until the top of the sixth, when Ronde came to the plate with two out and a man on third. After swinging and missing twice, he was so frustrated that he nearly threw his bat at the backstop fence. Luckily, he stopped himself, or he might have been thrown out of the game!

As he tried to get ahold of his emotions, a wild idea came into his head. If he couldn't hit a lick right-handed, he might as well give it a go *from the left side*!

As he crossed into the other batter's box, a chorus of shocked comments serenaded him from the Eagles' bench.

"What are you doing?"

"Ronde, no!"

"Are you nuts?"

"Hey, quit fooling around!"

Ronde was in a world of his own. He stared out at the pitcher, who wore a look of utter shock on his face. Standing in the left-handed batter's box, Ronde tapped the plate with his bat and waited.

The pitch came in—a searing fastball. And Ronde, who had no experience batting lefty—*ever*—simply reached out and let the bat touch the ball. It skittered down the third base line, staying just fair.

Ronde shot out of the box like a rocket, streaking toward first. The crowd was roaring, but Ronde saw nothing but the bag ahead of him. He crossed it just ahead of the throw, and kept on running down the baseline, clapping his hands because he knew the run had scored from third.

Tiki followed with a ground ball out, but the damage was done. "Man, what did you think you were doing?" he asked Ronde as they both ran to the bench to get their gloves.

"I have no clue," Ronde admitted with a laugh. "But I'm gonna try it again next time!"

In the bottom of the sixth, the Mountaineers came back against Ian Lloyd, the Eagles' relief pitcher, tying the game on three straight hits. The Eagles did not score in the seventh, and neither did East Side, so the game then went into extra innings.

And it kept on going. For two more straight innings nobody scored. But both relief pitchers were getting tired. In the top of the tenth, John Benson led off by grounding to short for the first out. Then Ronde came to the plate. Hitting lefty, he swung at the first pitch—and to everyone's amazement, including his own, he hit it sharply down the third base line for a double!

Now up came Tiki, Ronde took a big lead and gave Tiki a little nod as a signal that he was going.

On the first pitch Ronde took off for third. The throw came in a second too late—and now the Eagles were only ninety feet away from grabbing the lead.

Ronde glanced at the third base coach for the sign, and saw him touch his left ear, the sign for a safety squeeze play!

Ronde got ready. He knew Tiki would try to bunt the ball. Ronde's job was to take off for home on contact. He crossed his fingers, hoping that Tiki would indeed make contact. If not, there would be two strikes on him, and Coach would have to take off the squeeze.

Tiki's bat met the ball, and the ball dribbled right in front of the plate. The catcher got after it quickly and swung around to tag Ronde—but Ronde was too fast for him! He slid under the tag and his foot touched home!

Now it was 5–4, Eagles. But they still had three outs to get to nail down the victory. And both their pitchers were spent. Ronde saw Coach Raines tap Tiki on the shoulder. "You're on the mound," he said. "Let's go."

Tiki seemed like he was about to say something, but then he thought better of it. Nodding, he grabbed his glove and a ball and headed out to pitch the bottom of the tenth.

Ronde didn't have the best view from out in deep

center, but he could see that Tiki, who didn't know any trick pitches, at least had a decent fastball. He managed to strike out the Mountaineers' number nine hitter before issuing a walk to the leadoff man, who quickly stole second base.

The pressure was almost at boiling point now. Tiki walked the number two hitter, then fell behind 2–0 on the next guy. Two on, one out, and a very slim one-run lead . . .

Ronde could feel himself sweating from sheer nerves. He could only imagine how Tiki felt. He had only one pitch—the fastball—and he was just trying to get the ball over the plate so he didn't walk in a run!

It was no surprise when the hitter launched a screaming line drive in Ronde's direction. Ronde took off at a run, never taking his eyes off the ball. Luckily, he'd been playing deep, just in case. He reached the fence a second before the ball did. Planting one foot on the fence, he used the leverage to leap high in the air and grab the ball. The force of the line drive almost pulled him right over the fence, but he came down back on the field, with the ball still in his mitt. He turned and threw, but the runners were retreating anyway.

He'd saved the game! But there was still one out to get—the Mountaineers' cleanup hitter

The kid swung so hard at Tiki's first pitch that he nearly came out of his shoes. His second swing was even harder—the bat flew out of his hands and nearly hit the third base coach!

Now, they needed just one more strike. "Come on, Tiki . . . ," Ronde breathed. "Come on. Just . . . one . . . more . . ."

Ronde tried to visualize a fastball zipping past the bat and into the catcher's mitt. But Tiki had an even better plan. He acted like he was throwing his best fastball as hard as he could—but instead, he lofted a slow, lazy floater toward the plate.

The batter, who had started to swing at what he thought would be fastball, had to stop midswing. As he hesitated, the ball dropped in past him for a called strike three!

Ronde and the rest of the Eagles ran to the mound and mobbed Tiki. "I didn't know you had a trick pitch!" Ronde told him as they celebrated and their hard-won victory.

"Hey, bro," Tiki said with a huge smile, "neither did I!"

The final score was Eagles 5, Mountaineers 4. They'd gotten their second straight weird, strange, and thrilling extra-inning victory, and were back to .500 at last!

BROTHERS IN THE OUTFIELD

Tiki and Ronde arrived for practice, changed, and were ready to hit the field when Coach Raines called out from the door of his office, "Hey, Tiki, got a minute?"

Tiki and Ronde exchanged puzzled glances. Tiki said, "See you out there," and turned back toward the office. Coach Raines closed the door behind him and said, "Sit down."

Uh-oh, thought Tiki. He sure hoped this wasn't going to be another chewing-out session. He racked his brains to try to think of anything he'd done wrong. Other than a couple shaky throws from second that had almost sailed over the first baseman's head, he couldn't come up with anything.

"Nice job pitching the other day," the coach began. Suddenly Tiki had the weird thought that maybe Coach was going to make him a *pitcher*. Tiki barely had time to savor this enticing idea when the coach added, "You've got a strong arm. I've been thinking about it, and I'm not happy with Chris's arm strength in right. Too many teams are going first to third on us. How would you feel about switching positions for the next game?"

It wasn't really a question—it was a decision the coach had already made. That much, Tiki was clear on. He'd played on enough teams to know when coaches were really asking your opinion and when they were just trying to seem democratic.

"Whatever's good for the team, Coach," Tiki said, giving the correct answer to all such questions from coaches.

"Attaboy. Be sure you get some outfield practice before the next game. I'm excited to see how many long flies you and your brother can run down between you. And with that arm of yours, we're going to get some out-field assists from you, too, I'm sure." He offered Tiki his hand to shake, then said, "See you out there."

That was Tiki's cue to go. Back on the field, he met Ronde's inquisitive look. "He switched me to right field," he told his twin.

"What?"

"Yeah," Tiki said with a sigh. "He said it was because of Chris Jones's weak arm. But I kind of think it's because I was throwing wild at second."

"Well, it's not all bad," Ronde offered. "Just think— it'll be the two of us out there, side by side. The Barber brothers. That's a first for us in any sport!"

Tiki had to admit, it was an appealing idea when you looked at it that way. He decided to set aside his feeling that it was a punishment and go with whatever was best for the team. It wasn't just a mantra with him and Ronde. It was what they really believed, when push came to shove. Being all about the team had carried them to two straight state championships in football, and neither Tiki nor Ronde was going to change their approach now, so close to the end of their time at Hidden Valley.

The next afternoon the Eagles traveled to William Byrd Junior High to play the Badgers, a team that had been talked about before the season as a real powerhouse but that had started out 0–4. Either (a) they weren't as good as everyone thought, or (b) they were just about to break out and crush their next opponent. Tiki sure hoped it was a, not b.

The game turned out to be a slugfest and a nail-biter, with both pitchers giving up four runs before the third inning was over.

Tiki and Ronde were two for two, and each of them had made a nice play in the outfield, where a lot of Ian's pitches were being hit.

In the fourth, John Benson took over the pitching duties, and things got quieter. The score remained 4–4 into the bottom of the sixth, when with one out and men on second and third, the Badger's cleanup hitter launched a high, sinking fly ball to shallow right center.

Tiki took off after it like a shot. It was in the no-man's-land between right and center field, but he was the closest man to it. Just as the ball was about to fall into his glove, he got hit in the head, hard—so hard, he fell to the ground, seeing stars!

For a moment he didn't know where he was or what had happened. Then a second later came the realization that everyone was screaming.

The ball! Where was the ball? Tiki got up, looked into his glove, and saw that it wasn't there. He looked around and realized that Ronde was lying on the ground next to him, motionless!

But there in Ronde's glove was the ball! Tiki grabbed it and threw it in to second base, but he didn't watch its flight long enough to see if he'd doubled up the runners. Instead he kneeled down next to his twin and said, "Ronde! Are you okay? RONDE!"

"Oooohhhh," Ronde moaned, slowly opening his eyes, then squinting as the sunlight hit them. "Wha' happened?" Then, as he tried to sit up, "OW! My head hurts!"

"Mine too!" Tiki said. "We butted heads, yo. Are you okay?" He helped Ronde come to a sitting position, then saw that a welt was beginning to rise on his twin's forehead.

"Man, why didn't you call for it?" Ronde asked Tiki.

"It was my ball all the way!" Tiki replied.

"Mine too," Ronde said. "I guess I didn't think about who was playing right field."

"Same here. If I'd have thought about it being you in center, I'd have called you off for sure."

"No way. I would have called *you* off!"

That was the end of the argument, because at that moment Coach Raines, together with two or three other coaches from both teams, reached them and started checking to see if both boys were okay.

Tiki told them he was fine, even though his head did still hurt. But he could tell that Ronde was still shaky on his feet as they walked them both back to the bench.

"Did we get the out?" Ronde asked weakly.

"We got TWO!" Coach Raines said proudly. "You held on to the ball, and Tiki threw the runner out at second to end the inning. Best play of the whole season!" Still, Tiki could see the worry in the coach's eyes.

The two brothers sat on the bench and watched the rest of the game unfold, both of them holding ice packs to their heads.

In the top of the seventh, Ian Lloyd hit an incredible inside-the-park home run to give the Eagles the lead. Tiki tried to cheer, but his head hurt when he did, so he stopped. Ronde didn't even try. He still looked pretty woozy, in Tiki's opinion.

John Benson came on to get the Badgers out one, two,

three in the bottom of the seventh, and just like that, the Eagles were a winning team again!

Along with Ian Lloyd and Benson, Tiki and Ronde were the heroes of this game. But neither of the twins was feeling too great on this bus ride home. Tiki felt slightly nauseous and had a big ice pack tied to his head. Still, as bad as he felt right now, he was sure he'd be ready for the team's next game.

But sneaking a glance at Ronde, he wasn't so sure about his brother.

10

HEADACHES AND HEARTACHES

"Mom?"

"Yes, baby?"

Ronde knew she had to be worried about him if she was calling him "baby." She almost never did that anymore. Tiki had actually gotten annoyed with her once, a year or so ago, when she'd called him "baby" in front of their friends. So Mrs. Barber was careful about saying it—except for when she couldn't help herself.

Ronde saw that her eyes were filled with concern for him. "I'm okay. Really, mom. I could go to—"

"You can go back to school tomorrow, *if* the headache is gone. That's what the doctor said. So don't go trying to sweet-talk me into letting you get out of that bed."

"No, mom, you should go to work. I'm fine. Really."

"Put that ice pack back where it belongs," she ordered. "I already took the day off. I'm not taking any chances when it comes to my baby's brains."

Ronde sighed. He knew it would be no use to argue any further. Dr. Dreyer had given Tiki the okay to go to school, but he had ordered that Ronde be watched at least for one more day.

And both boys were forbidden to do any athletic activity for at least a week, when they would see the doctor again and be given clearance—or not.

Ronde didn't mind missing classes. His head ached too much to get any studying or reading done. But he did like watching game shows on TV, and he knew his mom would play cards with him if he got too bored.

But he hated to think what would happen to the team without him and Tiki. This was the worst possible time for the two of them to go down—and at the same time!

The Eagles were tied for second place in their division at 3–2, but they were about to face two of the best teams in the whole league, Pulaski and Patrick Henry. If the team lost both those games, they'd pretty much have to go undefeated the rest of the season to make the playoffs. And that was *if* Tiki and Ronde could come back after missing only two games!

Ronde adjusted the ice pack on his forehead, which was being held in place by a cloth bandage. His head hurt only a little now—not like the day before—and he suspected that at this point it was the cold of the ice pack that was hurting the most.

He thought about taking it off before the twenty minutes was up, but he knew his mom would somehow, with her uncanny sixth sense, know he had done it, and if she caught him cheating, she would make him start the twenty minutes all over again.

Not worth it. Ronde left the bandage in place and closed his eyes to wait it out.

Ronde couldn't bear to watch. Peeking from between his fingers, he saw the ball come down out of the bright May sky. He watched as seventh grader Jimmy Krupkowski, his substitute in center field, tried to find the ball in the blinding sunshine. Ronde only hoped Jimmy wouldn't get conked on the head by the ball. Three outfielders with concussions would be the absolute end of everything!

But no, the ball didn't hit Jimmy's head, or his mitt, either. It dropped right in front of him, and the Patriots' hitter raced around second heading for third. It took so long for Jimmy to locate the ball, what with everybody screaming at him from the bench and the stands, that the runner was halfway home from third before he even picked it up!

The score now read 9–4, Patriots. Ever since Ronde and Tiki had conked heads in right center, the Eagles' fortunes had taken a steep dive. The team had looked lost the previous week in getting thumped by Pulaski,

10–3 (They'd narrowly avoided the "mercy" rule, where the game ends early if one team leads by ten runs.)

And today the Eagles were getting relentlessly pounded by Patrick Henry. Jimmy had already made three bad plays and was oh for whatever, without reaching base even once so far in either of the two games.

Ronde felt sorry for him, but even sorrier for Tiki's replacement in right. Anthony Campbell was also a seventh grader. He had barely made the team and hadn't had any experience at all in game action.

Anthony, to his credit, would stop the ball from getting by him, even if he didn't catch it cleanly. But once he had it in his hand, he had no idea where to throw it! At least four times in the past two games, he'd fired the ball to the wrong base, or missed the cutoff man, or thrown it way wild.

It was hard for those two kids, and even harder for Ronde and Tiki. They had to sit there, powerless to help, while the rest of the team faltered. It was like watching a snowball falling down a mountain, slowly turning into a gigantic avalanche.

It was the sixth inning now, and the Patriots were really pouring it on. "Please, no mercy rule!" Ronde muttered to himself, hoping the Eagles could avoid utter humiliation. "Catch it, Jimmy!"

For once Jimmy seemed to hear him. He made a nice catch, and the inning was finally over. "Good job, dude!"

he told poor Jimmy as he came back to the bench.

Jimmy didn't smile back. "Yeah, for once I didn't mess up."

"Aw, come on now. You just need more experience is all. Look how fast you're improving!"

"Come on, Ronde," Jimmy said glumly. "I'll never be as good as you."

"Who says? And anyway, so what? There are plenty of guys I'll never be as good as. Just be the best you can be, Jimmy. Look, you're up this inning. Just forget everybody else around here, forget everything that's happened so far, and put the bat on the ball, okay? Finish the game strong."

The kid nodded. "Yeah, okay. I get you."

"You know I want to be back out there next game, but it might be you—so go up there and build for next time."

"Yeah. I will. Thanks, man," Jimmy said, grabbing his bat. "I appreciate that."

"No prob. Go whack that ball!"

Jimmy smiled as he strode to the plate. With a quick, short swing he smacked the first pitch down the right field line for a double. Standing out there on second base, he waved to Ronde and gave him a thumbs-up.

Ronde applauded. "Atta baby, Jimmy!"

"There you go," Tiki said, elbowing his twin. "I guess we can still help out, even if we can't go out and play."

Ronde nodded, allowing himself a small smile of satisfaction. "Yeah," he agreed. "But let's be honest, Tiki, if we can't get out on the field pretty soon, this team's not making the play-offs."

Tiki didn't answer, and Ronde knew his twin did not disagree.

"Well, boys," Dr. Dreyer said, putting away his instruments, "I don't see anything alarming going on. You're both sure there are no symptoms?"

Ronde and Tiki both shook their heads.

"Well, then, just be careful," he said. "Don't take any foolish chances out there. Any symptoms return, I want you to let me know immediately. Understood?"

"Yes, sir!" the boys said in unison.

"But, Doctor," said their mom, "are you sure? I don't want anything else happening to them."

"Mrs. Barber," said Dr. Dreyer, "your boys love sports. They love *playing* sports. If they're willing to hold back just a little bit to preserve their health, I'm comfortable with them being on the field.

"Yesss!" both boys said under their breath. Their mother turned around and gave them a stern look.

"I hope you hear what the doctor is saying," she warned them. "You don't take any chances. You don't 'take one for the team.' You don't go diving after balls. You don't go stealing head-first. You understand me?"

"Yes, ma'am," the boys said, nodding. And at that moment they meant it.

But Ronde wondered what would happen if he had to dive for a ball in the next game. If the Eagles' whole season was on the line, would he still remember his promise to his mother?

11

BACK IN THE GAME

The boys had counted on a raucous welcome when they returned for their next game with the Eagles. But they were taken aback when Coach Raines called them aside again, together this time, and gave them a stern lecture about always calling for the ball, and never assuming what the other fielder was going to do.

As if they needed the reminder! Tiki would never forget as long as he lived the sight of his brother, out cold, with the ball still in his outstretched glove.

Tiki and Ronde'd had lots of time to think about a whole bunch of things—about their approach at the plate, their positioning in the outfield, and most of all their team's dire situation.

The Eagles, after two losses when Tiki and Ronde had been sidelined, now stood at 3–4. There were five games left in the regular season, and *if* the Eagles won all their remaining games, they *might* still make the play-offs. It was a long shot, but it was still a shot.

But once the game got under way, the time for thinking was over. The Barber boys were all business, and so were the rest of the Eagles.

In their rematch against the Blue Ridge Bears, Tiki and Ronde were on base constantly—stealing, faking steals, forcing repeated pickoff throws, and taking the extra base on every hit. The Bears' pitchers were so distracted by the two of them that they wound up throwing meatballs to Ian Lloyd and Michael Mason, who soon had eight RBIs between them. Meanwhile, John Benson was throwing well, giving up only two runs in his five innings of work.

So lopsided was the game that it was called on the mercy rule after six innings, with the Eagles ahead, 12–2. Although Tiki hit no home runs, the Bears never could get him out. And aside from one ground out, Ronde was on base every at bat.

It was sweet revenge for the Eagles, who'd lost to the Bears in their second game of the season. But Tiki, Ronde, and the rest were just getting on a roll.

Two games later things were looking a lot more interesting. The Eagles had now romped to three straight victories against weak opponents—Blue Ridge, Martinsville, and William Byrd.

With two games left in the regular season, there was renewed hope at Hidden Valley Junior High. There was still a way into the play-offs—a narrow, long-shot hope. If the East Side Mountaineers lost this week to the lowly Blue Ridge Bears, and *if* the Eagles beat the mighty North Side Rockets, they were in! If the Eagles lost, though, or if East Side won, their slim hopes would get even slimmer.

The best team so far in either division, the Rockets were leading the North Division with a 9–1 record. They had beaten the Eagles in their first game of the season, but by only one run.

We can beat these guys! Tiki told himself as the Eagles got ready to take them on.

Dark clouds gathered in the sky, and the winds seemed to blow from every direction. "Think we'll get rained out?" Ronde asked him as they waited for the umps to signal the start of the game.

"I hope not. I'm psyched to go. Aren't you?"

"Uh-huh! We've gotta keep this roll going!"

"This is our day, dude," said Tiki. "Let's hush that crowd up, yo!"

Tiki stepped to the plate, primed for action. He could feel the energy coursing through his arms, and he nearly launched himself at the first pitch, which looked as big as a grapefruit heading right over the plate—but the pitch was a changeup, and Tiki wound up dribbling the ball right back to the pitcher for an easy out.

Tiki was disgusted with himself. Why had he forgotten everything Coach had told him? Why hadn't he waited and watched a pitch or two, to see what the guy was throwing?

He'd been too excited, too wound up, that's why. Tiki promised himself that, next at bat, he would stay totally calm and cool.

The Eagles went down in the first without a fight, as Lenny Klein and Chris Jones both popped to first base.

Luckily, Ian Lloyd was on his game, firing fastballs past three Rockets in a row for strikeouts.

The game stayed scoreless for three quick innings. Not a single Eagle reached first base. The Rockets threatened in the third but didn't score, leaving a man on third base when Tiki made a running catch of a windblown fly ball to right.

He ran back to the bench, traded his mitt for a bat and a helmet, and strode up to the plate, blowing out a deep breath. "Be calm. Stay loose. Wait for the pitch," he whispered.

The first pitch came in—another changeup. Tiki let it go by for strike one.

"Now I'm ready," he told himself. "Loaded for bear." But the next pitch was inside, and he was handcuffed— unable to adjust to the pitch's location. He knew he must have looked foolish with the weak swing he took.

Regardless, he was still up there, still had one more chance.

But now he was thoroughly confused. Was the next pitch going to be a fastball or a changeup? He couldn't guess, so he decided to just be ready for the fastball, and adjust to the changeup if he could.

It was a changeup. Tiki held back for a second, then swung as hard as he could. He felt his eyes close as he did so, and he knew he should be keeping his eyes on the ball. But it all happened so fast—a split-second, really—that there was no correcting his mistake.

"Stee-rike three!" the umpire called.

Tiki slammed the bat on the ground. "Hey!" Coach Raines shouted to him as Tiki sat back down. "Come on, Tiki, none of that. No wasted energy. You don't have to hit the ball all the way to China. Just see the ball and hit it. You're trying too hard, kid. Just let the game come to you, okay?"

Tiki wasn't sure what the coach meant by that last remark, but he nodded like he understood. He didn't want anybody to think he was stupid or anything. He sat on the bench and watched as the rest of the Eagles continued to swing and miss.

The game stayed scoreless through six tense innings. Both teams switched pitchers after five, but it looked like John Benson and the Rockets' reliever were being just as tough as the guys they'd replaced.

Finally Ronde led off the top of the seventh with a clean base hit to left.

"Yesss!" Tiki cried from the on-deck circle. "You're the man, Ronde!"

Ronde stared back at him from first, then cocked his head to one side. Tiki knew what the signal meant. It meant Ronde was going to take off for second, and that Tiki should take a pitch to give him a chance to steal the base.

Tiki let a big, slow changeup bury itself in the dirt at the catcher's feet, while Ronde took second base without a throw.

It was the Eagles' biggest threat of the game so far. Tiki swatted the next fastball the other way—right at the first baseman. The ball glanced off his glove and trickled toward the second baseman. By the time he picked it up, Tiki was at first, and Ronde had slid safely into third!

Still nobody out—but not for long. Lenny Klein struck out for the third time in the game, and so did Chris Jones.

With two outs now, and Ian Lloyd at the plate, Tiki decided to take matters into his own hands. Ian had already struck out twice today, and hadn't looked good doing it. The Eagles needed to score—it was now or never.

On the first pitch to Ian, Tiki took off like a shot. Glancing toward home as he ran, he saw the catcher spring to his feet and fire the ball toward second. Tiki knew his twin would use this chance to head home with the first run of the game.

The throw came in to second just as Tiki reached for the bag with his toe.

"SAFE!" the umpire yelled.

Tiki sprang to his feet and clapped his hands excitedly. It was 1–0, Eagles, on a two-out, two–Barber double steal!

Though Ian ended up striking out to end the inning, the Eagles entered the bottom of the seventh with that slim 1–0 lead. All they had to do was hold it—but something told Tiki it wasn't going to be so easy. . . .

Benson was throwing fireballs, and the first two hitters popped weakly to the infield. But then the Rockets' number three hitter looped a single in front of Michael Mason in left.

Then up came the cleanup hitter, and Tiki saw John Benson lick his lips nervously. "You got him, Johnny!" he shouted, but his voice was drowned out in the roar of the North Side crowd.

The count went to 2–0, but Tiki felt sure that the hitter was not looking to walk. He knew from recent experience that when you're a team's cleanup man, you want to knock that big run in yourself, not jog to first and leave it up to the next guy.

Tiki backed up a few steps in right, anticipating

trouble. He got it, all right—but not the kind he was looking for.

Benson threw a curve, and though the hitter swung for all he was worth, he didn't get good wood on the ball. It was a weak fly to shallow right center, and Tiki took off after it, remembering to yell "I got it!" over and over again.

At first it looked like he would get there in time. But just as he was closing in on it, he heard Ronde's voice over the roar of the crowd, shouting, "I got it! I got it!"

Tiki instantly pulled up short, thinking Ronde was about to crash into him again. Then, to his horror, he saw that his twin had done the very same thing!

The ball fell between them and skidded past into deep right center, where there was no one backing them up!

Tiki took off after it, and when he finally got to it, he threw it back in with all his might. But it was too late. Not only did the man on first score the tying run, but the hitter made it all the way around the bases for an inside-the-park homer, winning the game for North Side, 2–1!

Tiki sank to his knees in disbelief. Ronde came running up to him, saying, "You were calling for it! Why didn't you catch it?"

"Me?" Tiki shot back. "I heard you yelling, so I pulled up short!"

"But I heard you calling for it! That's why *I* stopped!"

Both boys sighed, realizing that their fear of another head-on collision had cost the Eagles a crucial game—and the team's best shot at the play-offs!

12

UP AGAINST THE WALL

"Check this out," said Tiki, showing Ronde the standings printed in the *Roanoke Reporter*. "East Side lost to Blue Ridge!"

"No way!" Ronde took a look and saw that indeed their archrivals had fallen to the lowly Bears, who even after their surprise victory had a 3–8 record.

Looking at the overall standings, Ronde saw that the North Side Rockets had clinched first place in the North Division, with a 10–1 record. The rest of the teams in that division were out of the play-offs, including two teams that were 8–3, better records than the Eagles'.

Luckily, Hidden Valley was in the South Division, where there were no powerhouse teams, and there was no clear winner yet. East Side was still on top, at 7–4, while the Eagles were a game behind at 6–5. The other teams in their division had losing records and weren't going anywhere.

"Am I reading this right?" he asked Tiki. "It looks like we've got our destiny in our own hands, right?"

With one game left in the regular season, the schedule had presented the Eagles with another gift—their final opponent just happened to be the very team ahead of them, the East Side Mountaineers.

If the Eagles defeated them, the two teams would have the same record—7–5—but the Eagles would win the division because they would have beaten the Mountaineers twice head-to-head.

Ronde grinned. He and his teammates could still squeak their way into the play-offs with only a 7–5 regular season record! "Wow. You know what, Tiki? We're still in this!"

Tiki elbowed him away from the paper to get a better look. "Out of my way. I've gotta see this."

"Hey!" Ronde said. "What's with the pushing and shoving?"

Just then their mom came into the kitchen.

"What in the world are you two fighting about?" she asked sternly.

"We're not!" Tiki explained. "We're reading the paper!"

"Looks like fighting to me."

"No, Mom," Ronde said. "We're looking at the standings."

"Don't you two have finals starting today? Seems to

me you ought to be studying every spare minute. I know you both know that your studies are more important than anything—including sports."

A brilliant flash crossed Ronde's brain. "We *are* studying, Mom!" he said, holding the paper up to show her. "See? Statistics! Math! Numbers!"

"And English!" Tiki chimed in, pointing to the paragraphs of text all over the page.

Mrs. Barber laughed. "All right, all right," she said. "I don't know why they let baseball season go so long, right into June. But as long as you two come home with good grades, I'm okay with it."

"We will, Mom," Ronde promised.

But a quick exchange of glances with Tiki showed him that his twin was just as worried about their upcoming finals as Ronde was.

They'd promised her As and Bs in exchange for permission to quit their part-time jobs at the department store so they could play baseball. It was costing the family real money too, because times were tight. Mrs. Barber had been working two jobs for the past year and a half.

As the boys rode their bikes to school, they didn't say a word. Each was absorbed in his own private thoughts.

Maybe we shouldn't have gone out for baseball after all, Ronde mused. If the Eagles missed the play-offs, he knew it would be as much his fault as anyone else's. Tiki's, too. If either one of them had caught that ball . . .

if he'd gotten just one hit, instead of all those strikeouts early in the season . . . and how about those boneheaded baserunning mistakes in their first two games?

He shook his head violently, to get those harmful, negative thoughts out of his head. This was no way to be thinking on the day of what might be their last big game at Hidden Valley! Whatever he'd done wrong up to now, he knew he and Tiki had also won a lot of games for their team.

And today they had a chance to win another one. If they could beat the Mountaineers, they'd have led their team to the division championship and the play-offs!

On the other hand, if they lost . . .

No! He couldn't let himself even think about it. He summoned back all the times in the past three years when he'd been in similar do-or-die situations. In almost every case, he and Tiki had come through and led the Eagles to victory.

Why should today be any different?

He would take the team on his shoulders, Ronde swore to himself, and lead them to victory . As he parked his bike, he remembered for the first time in many minutes that Tiki was right there next to him. The twins exchanged a serious, sober look, and Ronde knew that, as so often happened, their thoughts were running on parallel lines.

• • •

The English final was *haaaard.* Ms. Bernstein had fiend-ishly designed it to trip up kids who weren't paying the strictest attention during the test—or who hadn't been keeping up with the work all during the term.

There were right answers, almost-right answers, and sort-of-right answers. And then there was the *dreaded essay. . . .*

Essays were almost always the hardest part for Ronde. Funny, because when Tiki was writing the advice col-umn for the school paper, it was often Ronde's ideas he was putting down on paper. But when it came to actual writing, it was like Ronde's brain froze solid.

The topic for the essay was: "ARE CLICHÉS TRUE? Take a test case and prove your point."

They had learned about clichés, and Ronde in his recent studying had gone over them. They were phrases used so often that they were presumed true, but *were* clichés true?

Ronde tried to think of a good one. Ten minutes later he was still trying to think of one, and time was running short.

All day long he'd been trying to keep thoughts of baseball out of his mind and concentrate on the tests in front of him. It hadn't been easy in math, but at least that was his best subject and the answers were what they were—not vague or confusing. The answer was right or it was wrong—period.

Still, his mind had wandered a lot. Whenever a

number reminded him of his batting average, or the standings, or had any other connection with baseball, his brain would short circuit and the two sets of numbers would get mixed up.

That was hard, but he was pretty sure he'd done okay in the end, a B at least. With English, though, it was a different story. And this, as his mom had reminded him, was even more important than sports, at least at this point in his life.

Only five minutes left till the bell rang! He *had* to write this essay. He *had* to. . . .

Finally, a cliché came to him, and sure enough, it was baseball related: "It doesn't matter whether you win or lose; it's how you play the game." Ronde set to work, not even worrying whether what he wrote was any good—only that he wrote *something*. Handing in a blank essay page was not an option:

They say "It doesn't matter whether you win or lose; it's how you play the game." I think both are important. I guess how you play the game is *more* important, because that's all about what kind of person you are—are you kind, are you fair, are you brave, and can you master your own weaknesses. Stuff like that.

But anyone who says winning or losing isn't important hasn't got a clue what it's like to go out there and compete. If it weren't for winning and losing, playing the game wouldn't be half as much fun.

So I think it's not fair to say it doesn't matter if you win or lose. It matters. It matters to me right now, because I'm about to go out and play a game. If my team wins, we win the division championship and go to the play-offs. If we don't, my sports career here at Hidden Valley is over.

Oh, it definitely matters whether you win or lose. At least it sure does to me. And that's how I play the game.

He sure hoped Ms. Bernstein wouldn't think he was a sports-crazy jock and give him a C or a D. But the bell was about to ring, and he had a big game to play. It was time to switch gears. After handing in his test and giving Ms. B. a serious nod, he strode into the hallway and headed for the locker room.

• • •

As he pushed open the doors to the field and trotted out to join his teammates, Ronde felt like wild ferrets were having a wrestling match in his stomach. Normally on the day of a game, he spent every minute he could preparing himself mentally to go out there and play.

But today he'd been distracted by finals. They might have been more important than baseball, but they weren't going to help him play his best.

He blew out a few deep breaths and just sat on the bench, trying to compose himself. "You all right?" Coach Raines asked him, looking concerned.

Ronde nodded but said nothing. He just needed to concentrate, to get into his "game head." The other kids, including Tiki, were all out on the field, throwing the ball around, waiting for the game to start. But Ronde's nerves were threatening to make him "play tight," and he needed to just breathe . . . just breathe . . .

And then it was time to play. He grabbed his mitt and ran out to center field. Five minutes of concentrating his mind had given him a new burst of energy and focus.

He was ready now. "Bring it on," he muttered under his breath.

It was John Benson's turn to pitch, and that was a good thing. As well as Ian Lloyd had pitched, Benson had more speed on his fastball, and better control, too. They needed a good pitching performance today, and as Ronde watched, Johnny B. proceeded to strike out the side.

"Yesss!!" Ronde said, pounding his glove and head-ing for the dugout. He saw that Tiki was already grabbing a bat, and went over to him.

"This is it," he told Tiki. "We got this, yo."

"I know it," Tiki said, nodding. "You and me, Ronde. One more time."

They exchanged their secret handshake, and Ronde stood watching as Tiki went up to the plate.

13

MEN IN BATTLE

Tiki had only one thought in mind—to get himself on base. He dug his feet into the batter's box and got ready for the pitch. Glancing down the third base line, he saw Coach Barrett flash him the bunt sign.

As the pitch came in, Tiki squared around, and the ball hit his bat, but the bunt went skyward. Tiki muttered under his breath as he took off for first. He never stopped to see if the ball was caught in the air, but when the ump yelled "Safe!" he knew it had dropped before anyone had gotten to it.

Relieved, Tiki blew out a deep breath and took his lead as Lenny Klein stepped up to hit. Tiki knew how important it would be to get a lead on the Mountaineers. He'd seen their season statistics and knew that they gave up fewer runs than any other team in the league. In their previous meeting the Eagles had scored five runs, but that was the most East Side had given up in any game.

So Tiki set his sights on second base, with grand larceny on his mind. He had to get himself in scoring position. The problem was, the Mountaineers' pitcher was a fireballer who got the ball to the plate quickly. And their catcher had an unbelievable arm, strong and accurate. He'd thrown out almost half the runners who'd tried to steal on him (more statistics Tiki had found in the newspaper).

So Tiki tried to time the pitcher, watch what he was doing, and guess when he might throw a curve or a changeup.

The pitcher was clever. He would take a two-second pause before winding up, then before the next pitch, take a six-second pause. It threw Tiki off just enough to freeze him at first base while Lenny struck out.

With one out it was even more important for Tiki to steal. The sooner he got himself into scoring position, the more Eagles hitters would have a chance to drive him in. Chris Jones was given the *Take* sign by Coach Barrett, but he must have missed it, because he swung at the first pitch anyway and popped up to short for the second out.

"Dang!" Tiki muttered. He knew he'd better take off on the next pitch, no matter what. Ian Lloyd saw the *Take* sign and nodded to the third base coach. Tiki got the *Steal* sign, but he would have gone even without it.

As soon as the pitcher went into his windup, Tiki was off and running. He didn't even bother to look—he knew it would be a fastball, and he knew it would be bang-bang at second. He headed for the back of the bag, his feet pointing almost into left field.

The throw came in low, and the second baseman dug it out of the dirt. He swung his mitt around to tag Tiki—but Tiki was on the outfield side of the base. He reached his hand out, grabbed the corner of the bag, and held on to stop his slide as the tag hit him on the wrist.

"Safe!" the umpire yelled, and a roar went up from the Hidden Valley faithful.

It was strike one on Ian, but now Tiki was able to get inside the pitcher's head by faking a steal of third base. Twice the pitcher turned to fake a throw, and Tiki dove back. The third time, he actually threw—and almost threw it into center field.

By the time he got around to throwing to the plate, he'd lost his pinpoint control and walked Ian on four pitches. Up came Michael Mason, loaded for bear.

Tiki knew that the pitcher wanted to get the ball over the plate now, to get his third out—Michael Mason knew it too and was waiting for it. He ripped the first pitch —a fat fastball right down the middle—over the second baseman's head and into right field.

Tiki took off at the crack of the bat, and scored easily. Eagles 1, Mountaineers 0!

Cesar Ramirez was next up, but he quickly popped out to center, and the inning was over. Tiki was glad he'd been aggressive on the base paths. Without him causing mayhem out there, the Eagles would not have grabbed the lead.

This fact grew even more important as the game went on and both pitchers proved to be tougher than the hitters. By the third inning Tiki could tell that this was going to be a low-scoring game and that runs would be at a premium. With two outs, the Mountaineers tried to mount a rally. John Benson gave up a clean single to left, then walked the next batter. The Mountaineers' cleanup man hit a liner to center field.

"Get it, Ronde!" Tiki yelled. He watched as his brother took off after it. Ronde caught it, then stumbled and did a somersault—but he held on to the ball, and another loud cheer rose from the stands as Benson's shutout was preserved, for now at least.

Tiki breathed a sigh of relief. If that ball had been lined to Ronde's left instead of his right, he and Tiki would have been on another collision course. Tiki sure hoped that didn't happen again, today or ever. With two such speedy outfielders playing side by side, two guys who could run down almost any ball hit between them, you never knew what might happen—good or bad!

The score held until the top of the fifth. Benson was tiring now, and it showed. He didn't have the pinpoint control he'd had earlier in the game, and walked the leadoff man before going 3–0 on the next hitter. If he walked him too, it would be the Mountaineers' best scoring chance yet.

Knowing he had to throw a strike, Benson laid it in there, right over the heart of the plate. The hitter clobbered a liner right at Tiki!

Tiki froze in place, not knowing whether to head back on it or run in toward it. In the end he did neither. The ball was hit so hard that what he did was duck, holding his mitt up in front of his face to shield it from the missile.

POP! He heard and felt the ball smack into his glove— and miraculously, it stayed there! He'd caught it with his eyes closed!

He threw it back in, trying not to let his embarrassment show. Had anyone else noticed that he'd caught it only because he was protecting his face? He sure hoped not!

At any rate the momentum seemed to shift after his catch, because Benson got the next two batters to strike out and end the threat. It was still 1–0, Eagles, with only two innings to go to clinch their division, and a play-off spot!

Deep in his bones, though, Tiki felt sure that one run was not going to be enough for the Eagles. They needed at least one more, an insurance run that would give

Ian Lloyd a two-run cushion when he came in the next inning to close the game.

Ronde led off the Eagles fifth, still batting left-handed. Tiki shook his head and smiled every time Ronde got up there and stood in the wrong batter's box. Ronde had been right-handed all his life. He did everything that way—except for this one thing, and incredibly, it had been working for him!

The Mountaineers' pitcher had been mowing the Eagles down ever since Tiki's early run. Crucially, he'd kept the Barber brothers off base, allowing him to concentrate on the hitters at the plate.

It looked like this time would be no different. Ronde swung weakly at two blazing fastballs. Then he flailed wildly at a changeup in the dirt. "Strike three!" the umpire called.

But Ronde wasn't the only one who'd missed the ball. The catcher hadn't been able to haul it in either. "Run, Ronde!" Tiki screamed, along with a few hundred others.

Ronde took a second to get the message, but when he did, he was off like a cheetah. The catcher picked up the ball, fumbled it, grabbed it again, and threw—but the throw hit Ronde in the back and bounded away into foul territory. By the time the first baseman retrieved it, Ronde was on second base. And there was still nobody out!

Tiki watched admiringly from the batter's box as his brother started dancing off the bag at second. Tiki could see the pitcher frown, his jaw tighten, and his annoyance grow obvious. He threw a ball that came right at Tiki's head!

Tiki ducked out of the way, but the murmur and boos from the crowd seemed to only make the pitcher angrier. He blazed two fastballs right past the plate as Tiki watched, obeying the *Take* sign from Coach Barrett. Tiki understood. The coaches wanted to give Ronde a chance to steal third.

But the pitches were so fast that Ronde had no chance to move himself over. Tiki took a swing with two strikes, but the ball bounced right to the pitcher, who looked Ronde back to second before throwing Tiki out at first.

Tiki was disappointed in himself, but he knew this pitcher was one of the toughest in the league and had been all season. Besides, the coaches had given him only one swing at it.

The Eagles never ran a pitcher out there for more than five innings a game. But there were other teams in the league who let their pitcher go the full seven, even if it meant that, by rule, they had to use a different pitcher for their next game.

The Mountaineers were one of those teams. That was why the Eagles hadn't faced this pitcher the last time the two teams had faced off.

If Ronde couldn't shake this monster off his game now, who knew if they'd get another, better chance?

With Lenny Klein at the plate, Coach Barrett signaled *Take* again. Ronde started juking and jiving out at second base, clapping his hands and dancing on the balls of his feet.

Tiki saw the pitcher's jaw tighten, his face redden, and Tiki watched as the pitcher finally spun around and fired a ball to second base!

Ronde dove back headfirst, his arm outstretched, but the ball was fired so hard that it beat the second baseman to the spot. He couldn't grab it in time, and the ball sailed right into center field!

Ronde sprang to his feet and sped for third, and made it easily, although he did slide into the bag. He sprang up, clapping his hands and shouting, "That's what I'm talkin' about! Yeah, baby!"

Tiki whooped and hollered. "Go Ronde!" he yelled. He was so excited, he paced up and down in front of the bench as Chris Jones came to the plate.

Ronde took his lead off third base. He kept inching down the line toward home plate. The pitcher was now looking straight at him. Ronde kept juking and jiving, faking that he was going home, then dancing back a couple of steps toward third.

The pitcher got ready to deliver the ball. He stood in his stance, as still as Ronde was jumpy. Then, all at once, he took his foot off the rubber and flicked the ball behind Ronde to the third baseman, who was running for the bag!

Oh, no! Tiki thought. *He's gonna get picked off!*

And there was no doubt that he would have been, because the ball was at the bag long before Ronde would have gotten there—if he'd gone that way.

Instead, at the very moment the pitcher thought he was faking Ronde out, Ronde was pulling a double fake by heading straight for home!

Tiki was as shocked as everyone else. He stared in amazement as the third baseman turned and fired a rushed throw to the catcher, who was so shocked that he'd forgotten to throw off his mask. The ball came in at the same time Ronde did—and bounced off his helmet!

"Safe!" the umpire called. And just like that the Eagles had padded their lead to 2–0.

"Ronde, you rule! You do!" Tiki screamed, smacking his palm on his brother's helmet as Ronde basked in the glory of a team group hug.

"Let's go!" Ronde yelled. "Let's go, Eagles!"

The pitcher was obviously rattled. In spite of a mound visit from his coach, he proceeded to give up a base hit to Chris Jones to extend the inning. With Ian Lloyd up, Chris took off for second, trying to steal. He slid into the bag, and cried out in pain, grabbing his ankle. As he did so, he took his foot off the bag and was tagged out to end the inning.

The Eagles fans moaned in disappointment, then started to murmur worriedly as Chris limped off the field, favoring his left ankle.

"Tiki," Coach Raines's voice rang out. "I need you back at second for Chris. Jimmy, you're in right. Okay, let's go!"

As he settled in at second base, Tiki felt the anxiety rising inside him like the mercury in a thermometer. He had just been feeling really good about the team's two-run cushion. Now he found himself playing a position he hadn't practiced at for weeks, and had been demoted from for making too many errors!

At least that was how he'd felt when Coach Raines had switched him to the outfield. The coach hadn't said it was Tiki's poor play—in fact, he'd blamed it on the other kid's weak arm—but that didn't convince Tiki. He knew he'd made mistakes at second. It was a challenging position, where you had to react much faster than in the outfield.

As Ian took the mound for the top of the sixth, Tiki hoped that no balls would come his way these next two innings. His prayers were answered as Ian mowed down the Mountaineers, one, two, three.

In the bottom of the sixth, the Mountaineers' starter, still in the game, returned the favor. Incredibly, he was throwing harder now than at the beginning of the game. Three Eagles in a row whiffed on fastballs that Tiki, sitting on the bench, couldn't even see.

He trotted out to second again, knowing that this was it. The Eagles were three outs away from victory, from the division title, and from a play-off with North Side.

But he knew not to get ahead of himself. There were still three outs to get, and he knew the Mountaineers wanted this game as much as they did. They would not go down without a fight. He was sure of it.

"Don't let them hit anything to me," he muttered under his breath.

And wouldn't you know it—of course—the first ball hit was a grounder right at him! It was hit so hard that Tiki had to make a quick swipe at it with his mitt. The ball caromed off the glove and into right field as the runner continued all the way to second base.

It wasn't really an error. But it *felt* like one to Tiki. Sure, the ball had been hit really hard. Sure, it had hooked right toward him. It would have been a great play if he'd held on to it. And if he'd been a better infielder, he might have.

Oh, well, he thought. *No use crying over spilled milk.* He needed to keep his head in the moment, not replay what couldn't be changed.

Ian got the next hitter to pop up to Ronde, and struck out the man after that. Tiki was just beginning to think he might get away with his "error" with no harm done, when the next batter popped a ball up in his direction.

"I got it! I got it!" Tiki yelled, but there was no need

to, really. This was not the outfield. There was no one else who was going to have a chance at this ball.

It wasn't hit that high, or at all well. Tiki turned and drifted back on it, staring straight up into the sky—only to realize that the wind was pushing it back toward him and to his right. He tried to adjust but wound up turning the wrong way, and just missing it as the ball dropped to the ground.

The runner had been going with two outs and scored easily, while the hitter reached second without a throw. It was now 2–1, Eagles, with the Mountaineers threatening to tie the game.

Another error? Not technically, Tiki realized. But that didn't make him feel one bit better. He'd cost his team at least one run, and the threat wasn't over yet! There was another man at second, and he represented the tying run!

"Come on. . . . One more out, Ian. . . . Strike him out. . . . Stri—"

The ball was struck—another pop-up over his head. Tiki turned and ran back on it, already panicking. Was it possible he could make a third straight error and lose his team the game?

He felt dizzy, the world spinning as he tried to get under the ball in the swirling wind. Incredibly, it was blown back behind him, and he twisted himself around to get it, but missed!

He picked up the ball, crushed to have failed his

team, but then he heard Ronde's voice coming at him from center field and piercing through the noise of the crowd.

"He's going home! Throw it!"

Tiki turned and threw the ball to where he imagined home plate would be. (It all happened so fast, he never really got a good look.) The runner, it seemed, had hesitated, forgetting how many outs there were! Instead of breaking for home, as you would normally do with two outs, he had waited to see if Tiki would catch the ball!

That had given Tiki the chance he needed, and his strong arm did the rest. The ball popped right into Cesar's catcher's mitt on the fly, and the burly Eagles receiver tagged the runner on the helmet as he slid into the plate.

"Yer out!" the umpire roared.

The explosion of emotion was deafening. The Eagles' fans poured onto the field to celebrate. Their team had done it—the Eagles were South Division champs!

"Bring on the Rockets!" Tiki yelled as he and Ronde jumped up and down together.

"Yahoo!" Ronde shouted. "Play-offs, here we come!"

14

THE FINAL GAME

Ronde was studying that Saturday afternoon when Tiki walked into their room.

"What're you doing?" Tiki asked.

"What's it look like?"

"Poor Ronde, always studying. I'm sooo glad my finals are done with."

"Cut it out. It's not funny," said Ronde, feeling more than slightly annoyed.

"Don't you wish you could watch the ball game with me?" Tiki went on.

"Be quiet! Can't you see I'm—"

"Studying? Aw, poor you. Okay, bye. I'm going downstairs to watch the ball game. Bye. . . ."

"Why don't you work on your final advice column for the paper?" Ronde shouted after him, in one last desperate effort to ruin Tiki's good mood. Ronde kicked the door shut and sat back down at the desk. He wished that he were in Tiki's shoes, with all his finals done. He'd have teased Tiki about it exactly the same way, or worse, he knew. It would have been so much fun. . . .

He went back to his science textbook. Sighing, he turned to the page on gravity. The concept had been giving him fits for the past half hour. Try as he might, he couldn't quite get into his brain the fine points of how it worked.

Finally he slammed the book shut, got up, and pulled the door open. "You want me to come down there and watch the game with you?" he called out. "Then, help me with this stupid science final!"

Tiki was up the steps in no time. "Fine. As long as you're begging me for help . . ."

"I'm not begging," Ronde shot back. "If you want us to be able to get all As and Bs for Mom, you'd better help me on this, or else it's not gonna happen."

"Hmmm," said Tiki. "Well, when you put it like that . . ." He sat down next to Ronde and was soon explaining gravity to him.

"It's like the curveball, yo," he said. "It doesn't really curve, you know."

"What?"

"I'm serious. It doesn't curve."

"Then why do they call it a c—"

"Just listen, all right? It doesn't curve, but what

happens is, gravity takes over. The little ball gets pulled down by that bigger ball, Earth. Meanwhile, the ball has to fight its way through the air, which, even though the air is invisible, is there and pushing back, right? So the ball loses speed, and gravity takes over more and more, pulling the ball down toward the ground. Now add a little spin, and it changes the friction of the air and makes the ball go on a different arc. So if you're the batter, it looks like it's curving. Get it?"

Ronde frowned, blinking rapidly. "Incredibly, I actually think I do," he said. "Yeah. I do get it. Everything's always pulling on everything else, right?"

"Yeah!" Tiki said. "That's it!"

"Then why doesn't the whole universe just collapse in on itself?"

"Whoa. Dude," said Tiki, throwing up his hands, "that is way past my pay grade."

"Anyway," said Ronde, "it's a really good argument to make to Mom."

"Huh?"

"About how sports are good for your grades! You teach me about the curveball, and I get an A on my science final!"

Ronde aced his test on Monday morning. He got good news from his math teacher—a 96 on the final and a B plus in the course! And best of all, in English class, Ms.

Bernstein singled him out as she handed out grades.

"Ronde," she said, loud enough for everyone to hear, "congratulations. You are the first one in three years to get a grade of one hundred on one of my finals."

There was a collective intake of breath from everyone in the classroom.

"A hundred?" Ronde repeated, flabbergasted.

"That was the finest, most concise essay I've seen from a student in a long, long time!"

"My . . . essay?" He remembered it now. The one about how you play the game. He'd just tossed that off in desperation, without even thinking about it!

"You really should do more writing," Ms. B. went on. "You're very, very good at it!"

Shocked, Ronde had to consider the prospect. It gave him the shivers, but when he went home that night and read his essay over, he had to admit it wasn't bad at all.

Mrs. Barber was thrilled when she was presented with the boys' grades for the semester. Ronde had all As except for history, where he'd gotten a B, and math, where he'd gotten that B plus. Tiki got three Bs and two A minuses.

"We told you!" Tiki said to their mom.

"And you were right!" she said proudly. Then her smile faded. "It's just too bad that I'm not going to be able to make your play-off game."

"WHAT?" both boys said at once. They'd been really

looking forward to hoisting another trophy while she took their picture, just like they'd done after both football championships.

"I've got to work," she explained. "Mr. Howard needs me to do inventory. I'm so sorry, boys. We'll go out afterward to celebrate, okay?"

"Sure, Mom," Tiki said. He knew how hard it was for her. She was probably even more disappointed than they were. But he also knew that as they got older, and kept playing sports, they wouldn't always be near enough to home for her to watch them play.

He was going to miss those times when she could come watch. But he swore to himself that someday he would be able to bring her to all his games, no matter what it took.

The Eagles had started their season against these very same Rockets, and lost. They'd played them just a couple of weeks earlier, and lost again. So it was no surprise that everyone on the team was eager for revenge, and primed to play their best.

Unfortunately for them, so were the Rockets. They were all over John Benson's fastball like butter on toast. Before the first inning was over, they'd collected six hits and three runs.

John looked totally stunned as he plopped down on the bench. He was shaking his head in disbelief, but when anyone offered him encouragement, he just kicked the dirt at his feet in anger and frustration.

Not a good start. Ronde hoped that the Eagles' bats would prove equally red-hot. But the eruption in the top of the first seemed to have taken the wind out of their sails. Tiki was thrown out by a hair at first base, and Lenny Klein and Jimmy Krupkowski struck out swinging.

The second inning went just as badly. By the time the Eagles came up to bat again, the score was 6–0, Rockets.

Ronde shook his head in despair. How were they ever going to turn this game around?

"Inch by inch!" Coach Raines barked, as if he were answering Ronde personally. "One run at a time," he told his hitters. "Let's get back in this game! We can do this!"

But for all the encouraging talk, the Eagles went down one, two, three again. Yes, there was still time, but it was getting shorter and shorter.

At least Ian Lloyd kept the Rockets at bay in the third. His heroics in getting out of a bases-loaded, one out jam seemed to inspire the rest of the team, because in the bottom of the inning, they staged a comeback.

With one out John Benson singled to left. "Atta baby, Johnny!" Coach Raines yelled.

Ronde echoed, "Atta baby!" He was glad for John, who had looked tortured until that moment—tortured by the six runs he'd given up in just two innings of work the mound. Coach had made the right decision switch ing him to third base. Ian was pitching well, and it obviously wasn't John's day to contribute with his arm. Even so, he could obviously still contribute with his bat!

Ronde came up to the plate ready to swing. Down by six runs, there was no point in bunting. The situation called for base hits, and a lot of them! He let two pitches go by for strikes, because they were on the inside part of the plate and he was looking to go the other way, because that was how he felt comfortable from the left side.

Two balls and a foul tip later, he got the pitch he was looking for—a fastball high and outside—and he lashed it to left. Benson careened around second and slid into third ahead of the throw, while Ronde, seeing the opportunity, went all the way to second.

"Now we're cooking!" Coach Raines yelled, raising his hands over his head. "Come on, Tiki!"

Tiki strode to the plate, taking a couple of practice swings as he went. Ronde's eyes widened. Those were no ordinary swings, he realized. Those were home run swings. Playing to the situation, Tiki would be looking to launch one.

On a 3–1 count, the pitcher went with his best fastball. Tiki was ready for it. The bat hit the ball with such force that the ball seemed to rise in midair, gaining height as it went. *Hey!* Ronde thought. *What about gravity?*

Eventually the ball did come down, but it was way ver the fence, and when Tiki made it back to home plate, the Rockets' lead had been cut in half.

Best of all, they'd played only three innings!

Tiki accepted the mob scene that greeted him on his return to the bench. While that went on, the Rockets recorded the final two outs of the inning.

But that was okay, Ronde reasoned. They still had four innings to catch up. Three runs in four innings was not too much to ask, even against a strong pitcher like this one. The main thing was that Ian Lloyd keep throwing up zeros onto the scoreboard, keeping the game within reach.

Ian got out of the fourth okay, but he put two more men on base and threw a lot of pitches. Ronde glanced over at his twin, wondering if Tiki was going to wind up on the mound himself in the last inning because Ian was spent and John didn't have it today.

In the bottom of the fourth, the Eagles got another run back when Michael Mason hit a mighty blast that hit a car in the parking lot. It might have been the longest shot for any Eagle that year, at least when it counted. (Some of Tiki's batting practice blasts had gone even farther.)

It was 6–4, and in the fifth, Ian Lloyd finally seemed to find a rhythm on the mound, mowing down the bottom of the Rockets' order, one, two, three.

"Let's go, Eagles! Let's go!" Coach Raines practically

screamed, his face flushed with excitement.

Ronde came up with one out and nobody on. He knew how important it was for him to reach base in this situation. With Tiki up behind him, this might be the Eagles' last, best chance for a game-tying rally.

The first pitch was a changeup, outside. Normally Ronde would have let it go for a ball. But the pitch was up high, almost at his eye level, and Ronde knew he could slap it the other way. He reached for it, not trying to do too much—and the ball arced lazily over the third baseman's head and plopped down in shallow left field for a single.

Ronde clapped his hands and took a big, hefty lead. He wanted to go on the first pitch, because that would give Tiki more chances to drive him in from scoring position.

The pitcher surely suspected as much, because he threw over to first three times in a row, trying to pick Ronde off. On the third try Ronde got an idea. He said "OW!" really loudly, then got up and called time-out, limping around a bit to make the pitcher think he'd hurt his ankle.

Sure enough, the pitcher threw home on the next pitch, and Ronde was off and running like a rabbit being chased by a bullet. The catcher never threw the ball, so surprised was he. The pitcher threw his hands up into the air, knowing he'd been fooled by Ronde's act.

Never assume anything, Ronde said to himself. It was

a lesson the pitcher had just learned the hard way.

Now it was Tiki's turn to do his part. He took a couple pitches off the plate, and with a 2–1 count, smacked a fat fastball into the right center field gap for a double. Ronde scored easily, and the Eagles were only one run down!

Unfortunately, that was as far as it went, because after a walk to Lenny Klein, the next two Eagles struck out swinging. Still, there were two innings left. Still time to get that last run.

But did Ian still have enough gas left in his tank? He gave up a screaming liner to the first hitter, but Ronde ran it down at full speed for the out. Then Ian walked the next two hitters. Coach Barrett paid a visit to the mound, and that seemed to help, because Ian got the next man to ground to second base. Tiki, playing there for the injured Chris Jones, turned it into a beautiful double play, ending the inning.

The Eagles were flying high now. In the sixth they put their first two hitters on base, before Tyquan and John both popped up to the infield. Ronde came to the plate with two out and men on first and second.

The situation called for a base hit, or at least a walk that would bring Tiki up with the bases loaded. Ronde decided to take a pitch and see how things went. Unluckily for him, the pitcher threw a strike, to get ahead in the count.

That meant Ronde couldn't hope for a walk; he had to try to make solid contact. The next pitch was a ball, and he let it go. But then the pitcher threw an inside fastball that Ronde couldn't get around on. "Strike two!" the umpire cried.

Ronde fouled off two good pitches, then took one in the dirt. On a 2–2 count he saw an outside fastball coming and reached for it, hitting a soft line drive right between the shortstop and the third baseman!

As he rounded first, Ronde saw the throw come home. "Get down, Michael!" he yelled. "Slide!" Michael must have heard him, because he slid right under the tag. "Safe!" the umpire called.

They'd done it! The Eagles had come all the way back from 6–0 to tie the game!

Tiki followed Ronde's single with a long fly ball, but the center fielder caught it right in front of the fence. *So close, and yet so far,* thought Ronde. But never mind. It was a brand new ballgame now!

In the top of the seventh, Ian Lloyd began to tire. He got the leadoff batter on a great stab by Tiki of a line drive to the right side. But then he walked the next two batters, and Coach Raines walked slowly to the mound.

"Tiki!" he called, motioning for him to come in and pitch. Ian, kicking the dirt in frustration, walked slowly off the mound and took Tiki's place at second base.

Tiki took the ball from coach and said to him what Ronde imagined must have been something like, "Are you sure about this?"

The coach patted Tiki on the back and went back to the bench. Tiki threw a few warm-up pitches, and then the game resumed.

Ronde stood out in center field, watching his brother go to work on the Rockets' cleanup hitter. He poured two quick strikes in there, but then the hitter smacked a long fly to right field. Jimmy Krupkowski was out there in place of Tiki, who'd moved to second in place of the injured Chris Jones, and then to the mound in place of Ian.

Jimmy took off after the ball, and Ronde ran over to back him up in case Jimmy couldn't haul it in.

Jimmy hit the fence just after grabbing the ball. He fell to the ground, holding on to the ball, but Ronde knew that wasn't the end of the play. The runners on first and second might have tagged up and be heading home! He snatched the ball out of Jimmy's glove and threw it in to the cutoff man, who wheeled around and threw it home.

Sure enough, both runners had tagged up. The ball beat the runner to the plate, and Cesar put the tag on him. "Yer out!" called the ump.

"Fantastic play, Jimmy!" Ronde said, helping his teammate up and slapping him on the back. "See? I told you you had it in you!"

Now there were two outs, with a man on second. One more out, and Tiki would have gotten through the inning unscathed. But the next hitter connected on a weak fly ball to right. It was not hit very well, and the ball didn't go very high, but it was perfectly placed. It fell between Jimmy, who had been playing deep, and Ian, who'd been guarding second base so the runner wouldn't get too big a lead.

That runner, with two out, had been off at the crack of the bat, and when the ball fell in for a hit, he was already around third and coming home to score the go-ahead run!

A loud moan went up from the Eagles and their fans in the stands. After such a great comeback, were they destined to come up one run short after all?

Tiki seemed to channel all his frustration into his pitches to the next batter. He'd almost done it, almost gotten the team through to the point where they could take the championship. But one stupid, weak little hit had done him in! His anger gave his arm extra oomph, and he blew three straight pitches right by the hitter to end the inning.

Now it was all up to the Eagles. Could they mount one last rally?

With Chris Jones out, the Eagles had Lenny Klein, Michael Mason, and Cesar Ramirez coming up. Three good hitters. And the Rockets had a new pitcher on the mound. Maybe he'd be off his game, or easier to hit than their starter.

The new guy was not overpowering. Ronde could tell from his warm-up throws. He wished he and Tiki were about to get up to the plate against him. But those slow, tantalizing pitches seemed to mesmerize the Eagles' hitters. Lenny whiffed at two pitches before looking at a third strike. "What?" he complained when the ump called him out, but the ump just repeated, "Stee-rike three! Yer out!" and gave Lenny a look that said, *Don't argue with me.*

"Come on, Jimmy!" Ronde yelled, cupping both hands to his mouth like a megaphone. Jimmy Krupkowski was a big kid, even if he was a seventh-grader. If anyone could tie this game with one swing of the bat, it was him.

But Jimmy's mighty swings caught only air. This pitcher wasn't so easy to hit after all, Ronde was realizing. There was a method to his madness, throwing up pitches that looked easy to hit, and making the Eagles hitters swing too hard, or too early. He went from slow, to slower, to slowest, and Jimmy went down in futility. He had swung three times—hard enough to drive a ball all the way to China—and hadn't hit a thing.

Now the Eagles were down to their last out, with Ian Lloyd at the plate. Ian was a powerful kid, and certainly had strength enough to hit a ball out. But he was far from fast. When he hit a ground ball to third, Ronde held his breath. And when the throw was true, and the first baseman had it in his mitt, Ronde let the breath out.

The final breath of ultimate defeat.

The Eagles had lost, 7–6. It was all over. All of it. The

season, their careers at Hidden Valley—everything.

Ronde couldn't believe it. It was like walking in a dream. The silent crowd sat stunned, as if there were still more baseball to be played.

Ronde looked for Tiki but couldn't find him at first. And then he saw his twin, leaning against the backstop, his glove dangling from his hand. Tiki looked like he'd just been hit with a brick.

15

SILVER LININGS PLAYBOOK

When the ball settled into the Rockets' first baseman's mitt, when it was finally over, it was as if the world stood still. Tiki went into a crouch, wrapped his head in both his arms, and felt it all hit him like the blast from an explosion.

There were cries of joy from the mound, where the small knot of Rockets players were celebrating their championship season. Otherwise the field and stands were quiet. Nobody said much. There wasn't much to say.

It was all over, Tiki thought. Everything. His and Ronde's dream of going out on a high note, a glorious exit from Hidden Valley Junior High . . . everything. Finals were over, sports were done for the year. A long, sad summer awaited them. Plenty of time to dwell on this bitter, final defeat.

In the locker room Coach Raines spoke to his disconsolate team. "I'm proud of you boys, each and every one of you," he said, his voice full of emotion. "You battled, you came back from injuries and defeats, and you came within one run—one run!—of getting there. Sometimes the ball bounces into your mitt and you win the game, and sometimes, it takes a bad hop and you lose. I know that for most of you this is it for your careers here. I just want to say that it's been an honor and a pleasure to work with each and every one of you. And for those of you coming back, I just want to say, wait till next year."

They all applauded, and as the applause was dying down, Ian said, "Let's hear it for the coaches!" and that got a big, hearty cheer.

Most of the kids seemed to lighten up a bit after that—except for poor John Benson, who'd been so great all season on the mound, only to cough up six runs when it mattered the most. John seemed inconsolable, sitting on the bench and staring at the floor with his elbows on his knees and his chin in his hands.

"Yo, Johnny," Tiki said, sitting down next to him and putting an arm around his shoulders. "Not your fault, man. We lost this as a team."

"We did not," John muttered, not looking up. "It was me. That's all there is to say."

"No, man!" Tiki argued. "Remember when Ronde and I messed up that fly ball? If that had been today instead of a couple games ago, you could have said the same about us! We got here as a team, and we fell short as a team."

John looked up at Tiki now and nodded slowly. "Yeah, I guess that's true." He sighed. "But why today? Why did I have to mess up in the biggest game of my life?"

"Hey, every game's got a winner and a loser. It was just our turn to be the losers today. It's not the end of the world, yo."

And as he said it, Tiki realized for the first time that day that it was true. It wasn't the end of the world—only the end of their time at Hidden Valley Junior High.

Later, when most of the players had already left, and as Tiki and Ronde were stuffing team equipment into duffel bags, delaying their inevitable final exit, Coach Raines came over to them.

"I just want to say, to you two boys in particular, how much I've enjoyed coaching you," he said. "You gave this team the best chance it's had in five years to win a championship. We would never have made the play-off without you."

"Hey, we were just doing our part," Tiki said. "Everybody had a part in it."

"I also appreciate the leadership, and the attitude you brought to the clubhouse. You showed these kids there's no *I* in 'team.'"

"Thanks, Coach," Ronde said.

"I see a bright future for the two of you," the coach added. "Don't ever change the way you go about your business. You're real winners, and I mean that sincerely."

They shook hands with him, and the twins slowly made their way back onto the field, for one last look before leaving.

Jason Rossini was waiting for them. "Hey, I thought you'd never come out of that locker room!" he said, a bit too cheerfully. "How does it feel to come out on the short end for once?"

That stung Tiki, and he felt like saying something mean right back, but he held his tongue, and so did Ronde.

Finally, as Jason kept at it, Tiki found the words he'd been looking for. "You know what?" he said. "I'm not sorry we went out for baseball, not for one second. It was all worth it, the winning and the losing. We had a great team, and we went into battle together. I'm glad you came home with a trophy, Jase, but we've already got a couple of those. This time we had a chance to play baseball, something we've always wanted to do but never got to. We might never get to again either. So it was definitely worth it, even though we didn't come out on top."

"And we made some new friends, too," Ronde chimed in. "Like Johnny B. and Jimmy the K. You make any new friends in track, Jason?"

"Aah, you're just looking for silver linings, the two of

you," said Jason. "See you over the summer, huh? Tell you what? We can have a race of our own. Me against the two of you!"

"You're on, yo!" Ronde called after him. "We'll leave you in our dust!"

"Ha!" Tiki laughed, appreciating Ronde's pride in their speed, and in the way they lived their lives.

Still, as the school year ended and the long summer days yawned ahead of them, both boys started to get down in the dumps. And then, one day in late June, they were walking past the high school when they heard a familiar voice calling their names.

"Hey, Ronde! Tiki!"

"Coach Spangler!" they cried out in unison, recognizing their old coach as he came walking toward them.

"Hey, boys, how's it been going?" he asked, shaking their hands and clapping them on the shoulders. Coach "Spanky" Spangler had been coach of the football Eagles when the Barber twins had first arrived at Hidden Valley. Under his guidance they'd improved a lot as players, even though, as seventh graders, they hadn't seen much game action. Later, though, after Spangler had moved on to coach at Hidden Valley High, they'd gotten to know one another better. The coach had followed their football careers as they'd led the Eagles to two straight state championships.

"I saw the baseball play-off," he told them, surprising both Tiki and Ronde.

"You were there?" Ronde groaned. "Oh, man, that was a terrible day."

"Not at all!" Spangler disagreed. "You guys played a heck of a game. That other team had an 11–1 record going in, you know. You guys were underdogs from the start."

"I guess," Tiki said. "Still, it didn't feel very good to lose."

"Of course not!" Spangler said. "You wouldn't want losing to feel good, would you? That's what gives you the urge to win! So, listen. I've been thinking of giving you guys a call."

"Us?" Ronde said, surprised.

"Yeah. You know I've got freshman slots for you on the team."

"You mean we're going to be starters?"

"Well, I don't know about that, but you're gonna be in there every game, playing significant minutes, even as freshmen."

"Wow!" Tiki said excitedly. He'd been expecting to ride the bench, like in seventh grade. It was what the new guys on the team always had to do.

"You've shown enough talent these past three years to deserve a starting spot, but of course the seniors have to get those spots, at least at the beginning of the season.

But never mind. You're going to play a lot, boys. And I want you to be ready. So this summer I was thinking it might be good to have you come in two or three days a week and work out with some of the starters. In fact, Matt Clayton's going to be there too. He's taking over at QB this year, so you guys can get reacquainted."

"Matt Clayton!" Ronde repeated.

Matt had been their first friend on the Eagles when they'd arrived as seventh graders. He'd been the star quarterback back then, and he'd made sure the Barbers were accepted by the regulars on the team. Because of him they'd made friends with everyone else right away, and felt like part of the team, even though they hadn't been getting to play much.

"He's excited to be working with you guys again. He told me to tell you to bring your A game with you."

"No problem!" Tiki said.

"So, you're up for being part of it?"

"Sure thing!" Ronde said.

"And how!" Tiki agreed.

"Great. We start on Monday. Be there at ten a.m., okay?"

"You got it, Coach!"

Tiki and Ronde turned to each other and exchanged their secret handshake. "Yesss!" Tiki said. "This is going to be awesome!"

"I can't wait for Monday!" Ronde said, his grin stretching from ear to ear.

All thoughts of their defeat on the baseball diamond flew from their heads. After all, football was, and always would be, their first love. And based on what Coach Spangler had said, their football future was as bright as could be.

Their ultimate dream, of playing in the NFL, was still alive and well. In fact, their dream was better than ever, because by playing other sports, like basketball and baseball, they'd learned a ton about things like leadership and teamwork.

"Man," Tiki said, feeling the glow of excitement fill him from head to toe. "I can't wait for September!"

"Me too!" Ronde agreed. "Look out, Hidden Valley High School, 'cause here we come!"

BASEBALL TERMS

Ball: A ball is called when the pitcher throws a pitch out of the strike zone and it is not swung at by the batter.

Bunt: This is an offensive play where the batter intentionally taps the ball to the infield. A pitch is usually bunted when the batters goal is to get on base or advance another runner into scoring position.

Double play: This is a defensive act in which two offensive outs are played one right after the other in one continuous action.

Fly ball: Also known as a pop-up, this is a ball that is hit high into the air.

Grand slam: A play in which the batter, while having men on first, second, and third base, hits a home run to bring in a total of four runs.

Ground ball: A ball that is hit and skips close to the ground.

Home run: A play in which the batter can make it around the bases and back home without being called out. This can be either an out-of-the-park home run or an inside-the-park home run.

Line drive: A ball that is batted in the air but not high off the ground.

Pinch hitter/runner: An instance where a substitute hitter or runner replaces one of the players in the game. Pinch hitters or runners usually replace the existing player because the coach believes the substitute has a better chance at scoring.

Stolen base: This is a play where a runner on one base successfully advances to the next without the batter hitting the ball or getting walked. A base is usually stolen to place runners in scoring position.

Walk: A batter is walked when four balls are called. Sometimes batters are intentionally walked when the pitcher feels he has a better chance at getting the next batter out.

Wild pitch: A ball that is pitched too high, too low, or too off to either side of the strike zone to be controlled by the catcher.

ABOUT THE AUTHORS

Tiki Barber grew up in Roanoke, Virginia, where he wore number 2 for the Cave Spring Eagles during junior high school. From 1997 through 2006 he wore number 21 as running back for the New York Giants, where he holds every rushing record in team history. He lives in New Jersey.

Ronde Barber wore number 5 for the Cave Spring Eagles. He wore number 20 as one of the top cornerbacks in the NFL for the Tampa Bay Buccaneers until he retired in 2013. Ronde is a Super Bowl champion and was selected five times for the Pro Bowl. He lives in Florida with his wife, Claudia, and their daughters.

Tiki & Ronde Barber have collaborated on nine other children's books: *By My Brother's Side*, the Christopher Award–winning *Game Day*, *Teammates*, *Kickoff!*, *Go Long!*, *Wild Card*, *Red Zone*, *Goal Line*, and *End Zone*.

Paul Mantell is the author of many books for young readers, including books in the Hardy Boys and Matt Christopher series.